LATE LIFE

Late Life

An Oklahoma Story

RANDOLPH FEEZELL

Fine Dog Press

To My Wife, Barb, Bugette Extraordinaire

Some memories are realities, and are better than anything that can ever happen to one again.

-Willa Cather

CONTENTS

PROLOGUE

It was late spring when I received the call, a familiar voice I had not heard for many years. It was Ruth, my high school friend, a younger sister I never had, telling me the bad news. Josh, her older brother, my classmate at Conway High School, one of my best friends in those pregnant times, died. Benign skin lesions, minor irritants, had turned deadly. Ruth thought I would want to know. Perhaps I could return for the funeral? Unfortunately, a long trip wouldn't be possible at this time of year, I said. I expressed my deepest regrets and my memories began to percolate wildly.

I had loved the Kirchner family – and Josh held a very special place in my past, at the conjunction of two dominant themes in my childhood: baseball and religion. Josh was there at the center, with Pastor Fred and Jake and Coach Ross. I had moved on from Conway, Oklahoma, but it had never moved on from me.

Ruth and I chatted for a while, tried to talk about the present, but the past kept getting in the way. Do you remember...? I told her I had been thinking about writing the story of my high school years but I wasn't sure anyone would want to read it.

"Write it for me, Lizzie. I didn't always understand what was going on. After you left I wondered what had happened. But I knew you were strong. Tell your story, Lizzie. Tell it for me."

I told Ruth I would have free time in the summer. I was between projects. I might be able to complete a short manuscript by late summer or early autumn.

"Have you told Chance about Conway?"

"Not much."

"Then write it for him, also. He's old enough to understand."

Yes…he is.

A few months later I sent Ruth the first draft of my manuscript. I hoped she would understand the title.

| **one** |

Jesus Christ and the St. Louis Cardinals

My father was raised in a small town in southeastern Missouri. (That's muh-ZER-a.) There were two ruling passions in his family: Jesus Christ and the St. Louis Cardinals. Two religions: one supernatural, the other as natural as Stan "the Man" Musial's swing and Lou Brock's speed.

One of my father's theological influences proved to be enduring in my life; its deepest rituals are as much a part of me as my memories and inclinations. It's a religion that taught me about faith and humility as each winter turned into spring. I learned not "to get the Big Head," as Pastor Frederick Lee Ware (Fred, my father) taught me, and that "whosoever shall exalt himself shall be abased, and he that shall humble himself shall be exalted." Humility before God? No, humility inscribed in the unwritten Good Book of Baseball. The percentages are against even the best and most virtuous; the possibility of suffering (striking out with the bases loaded) haunts the demi-gods who are chosen. We must be prepared to fail more than we succeed, and if we flourish, it's often more a matter of luck than will – a blooper sometimes turns into a hit.

My father's hometown was situated at the cultural confluence of Kentucky, Tennessee, and Arkansas, more self-consciously southern than midwestern. I failed to escape those influences as well. We carried them to the plains of Oklahoma as I grew up. Breakfast was served with grits, the okra was fried, and the tea was sweet.

Our talk was southern, slower than midwestern or yankee speech, with distinctive pronunciations: the charming inefficiency of transforming a one syllable word into two syllables, as in "oi-yul" (oil), "day-unce" (dance) and "dray-us" (dress); an emphasis on the first syllable in words such as "SEE-ment (cement) and "IN-surance (insurance); the vanishing (that's "vanishin") "g" in every "ing" ending. There were patterns of rural familiarity and formal expressions of respect for elders: "yes MAY'-am" and "No sir."

It was inevitable that my parents' southern way of talking would seep into my speech. Years later when I entered the highfalutin world of higher education, our singular "y'all" got me in trouble. I asked one of my professors, a formal, frigid fellow, about his garden. Full of insider experience gleaned from my parents' small vegetable gardens, I asked: "What do y'all have planted?"

He paused, stared at me, and pierced my low-brow soul. "WE-all have a variety of vegetables planted here."

Sorry for my red dirt talk. I wanted to slink away, thoroughly chastised, my backward roots unearthed. It was high-brow bullying, intended to put me in my place, make me feel small and uneducated. But I learned something that day – about academic prejudice, male chauvinism, and power. In the future I tried to make my talk unlocalized, as bland as a turnip – not a "y'all" to be heard, but vestiges of southern-ness remained throughout my life.

My father was an excellent three-sport athlete in high school, six feet tall, slender, black hair combed high in front, handsome, and fast. He was an all-everything baseball player, good enough to play at a small Methodist college in Missouri until the war broke out – which turned out to be the end of his baseball career, as well as the beginning of his gap years, until he could return to college and finish his degree after the war.

He served on the USS Woodworth in the South Pacific, participated in battles, including the Battle for Leyte Gulf in October, 1944, and kept a list of the Woodworth's successes in fighting the enemy: "17 planes, 2 subs, 3 cargo ships, 2 destroyers, 13 opposed bombardments, 27 shore batteries destroyed."

Fred left the USN on October 19, 1945, finished his degree in 1946, and married his high school sweetheart, my mother, Jean Ware (nee' Kamas). At this point in his life, he explained, my father felt the Call to the ministry. He attended seminary, was ordained, and assigned to his first church. I arrived as an early Christmas present in December, 1949, a baby boomette, destined to be an only child – and a preacher's kid.

One of the reasons I can recount these elements of my father's life is because I heard them, straight from the pastor's mouth. He was a storyteller. His narrative gifts made him an entertaining father and an engaging preacher. He told me stories about his childhood, the courting of Jean Kamas, the war, the Bible, and the St. Louis Cardinals.

As he told it, the radio helped turn the Cardinals into a regional obsession, not merely a big-city distraction from the Depression. My grandfather took Fred to his first Big League game in Sportsman Park in 1934, the year Dizzy Dean won thirty games and the Gas House Gang won the National League Pennant. He told me stories about Johnny Mize and Ducky Medwick, who won the Triple Crown in 1937.

Fred's favorite player in the 1940s wasn't Stan Musial, whose career began in 1941 and lasted until 1963, with a war year hiatus in 1945. All of Musial's MVPs and batting titles couldn't surpass the thrill of Enos Slaughter's famous "mad dash" in the 1946 World Series.

He tucks me in and I ask him to tell me a baseball story. (No Bible story tonight.) "Tell me the one about Enos Slaughter."

"Well, Lizzie, it was just after the war, in 1946. I was tryin' to finish college and I had married your mom that summer. The Cardinals won the National League Pennant but they had to face the Boston Red Sox, who had the great Ted Williams playin' for them. The Red Sox were big favorites. The Cardinals hung in and pushed the series to game seven. It was 3-3, bottom of the eighth, two outs. Enos Slaughter was on first base. He was a tough, gritty, hard-nosed player, and a Methodist, Lizzie, just like us, but from North Carolina. Lifetime .300 hitter, right on the nose. He was fast, but not fast enough to score from first base on what should have been a single. Harry Walker was at the plate. The count was 2-1. That's a good count to hit-and-run, because the other team probably won't pitch out. (I nodded, knowingly). The manager calls for the hit-and-run. Enos Slaughter takes off with the pitch. Walker lines the ball into left-center field, it's scooped up, and the outfielder relays the ball to the shortstop, Johnny Pesky, who figures that Enos will stop at third. The third base coach puts up his hands, palms up, like this. (Fred shows me the stop sign.) But Slaughter is flyin' around third, right through the coach's stop sign, and everybody is surprised, including Pesky. Here comes Enos, barrelin' toward home, Pesky throws, and the ball should'a beat him. Nobody scores from first on a single. The crowd roars, the runner slides...he's safe!" Fred flamboyantly gives the umpire's safe sign.

I think Fred loved the 1940s Cardinals best: Mort and Walker Cooper, Marty Marion, Stan Musial (of course), Red Schoendienst, Max Lanier, Whitey Kurowski. He described players as if they were his best friends. They became my imaginary friends when he told me baseball stories.

A big change occurred for the Ware family in 1953, when the Anheuser-Busch brewery purchased the St. Louis Cardinals and August "Gussie" Busch Jr., a beer baron, became the president of the club. Sportsman Park was renamed Busch Stadium and the Cardinals became associated with a brewery and the Sultan of Suds (as he was called).

For my father's family and many of his upright friends, at least those whose relationship with Jesus was dry, there was a big problem brewing. How could they support a team whose ownership was soaked in booze? For the sake of their faith, shouldn't they root for another, less boozy team?

The problem was especially acute on Sundays. The deepest weekly moral dilemma was on that day during baseball season, because keeping the sabbath holy was in apparent conflict with seriously supporting the Cardinals, listening to their games broadcast on KMOX radio in St. Louis. The Ware's brand of Methodism frowned on fun, in general – very surprising, given my father's athletic background, which, in my opinion, is all about having fun – and anything having to do with alcohol, in particular.

For Fred, baseball was a form of tribalism, a congregation of adherents to Cardinalism, unified by muscular and virtuous responses to the hated Chicago Cubs, the Cardinals' biggest rivals.

The Cardinal broadcasts were full of reminders that Fred's Christian integrity was at issue when rooting for the guys with "two birds on the bat." The broadcasts were full of advertisements selling beer. Christian fans were suspicious of play-by-play announcers whose words were slurred by the late innings. If the microphones were situated just so, listeners could hear the beer man calling out, like an evangelist at a revival: "Ice cold beer here! Beer here! Ice cold beer! Get your beer here!"

My father tried never to miss a game on the radio. On Sundays the transition from the pulpit and pews to the festive atmosphere of the stadium, set apart from God's less fascinating world of sin and work and bills, was a religious overload for the devout. Others in the community of believers (in Jesus and the Cardinals), including Fred, had rationalized their devotions by offering a creative interpretation of Sunday baseball. These games were really celebrations of God's gifts to his creatures. Budweiser need not spoil their appreciation of God's bounties.

At some point, when my father tried to explain his thinking, I was impressed by the ingenuity of Methodists who juggled their life in two worlds: one defined by a stern and sober love of Jesus and a biblical way of life; the other a secular domain awash in sinful behavior and fun. Fred wouldn't go into a bar or restaurant that served liquor, but he had successfully negotiated the problem of a teetotalling love of the beer-soaked St. Louis Cardinals.

I recall sitting in the stands between Fred and Jean, the beer man in the aisle to our right. He hands two cold Buds down the row, directed to a couple of customers to our left. Problem: Fred and Jean wouldn't touch the bottles. They were passed awkwardly across the Wares from the person on my mother's right, past our three seats to a fan on my father's left.

Among my earliest childhood memories are our summer trips to relatives scattered in Tennessee, Arkansas, and Missouri, always combined with a pilgrimage to St. Louis to watch a weekend of Cardinal games, including a Sunday doubleheader if we were lucky. Fred took me to my first games in Busch Stadium before I learned to play catch.

Three good tickets, a few rows up from the field along the first base line. The jostling energy of the fans as we enter the lower grandstand. Up the ramp and a first sublime picture of the enormous enclosed space. The expanse of vivid green, the deep umber of the infield dirt, the four shining bases defining a geometric perfection, the low hum of the crowd's excitement as the players take their final warmup throws in the outfield, the deep reverberating public announcer telling us to get our scorecards ready for "today's lineup."

Fred kept score as he tried to concentrate on the game, pitch by pitch. He explained to me what was going on and how to symbolize it on the scorecard.

The scorecard was a collection of squares to be filled with numbers, letters, lines, and abbreviations. I learned that 6-3 was a groundball to shortstop, who threw to first base for the out. F9 was a flyball to right field. A half diamond from home to second base, along with a 2B, meant that a batter had hit a double. If a runner scored, Fred would fill in the diamond with the little yellow pencil that came with the scorecard. Later I learned that Fred's method of keeping score included some idiosyncrasies that "just made sense," as he said. The goal was to represent a game concisely and accurately on the scorecard.

When I became adept at this mode of abstract representation, we both kept score. Fred compared our scorecards after a game. Then he quizzed me. "What did Musial do when he batted in the seventh inning? Did he get an RBI? What pitcher gave up the hit? Who scored on his hit? When did the Cardinals hit-and-run? Who was the runner? Who was the hitter?"

When I held the finished product I was satisfied that a game could be depicted so cryptically – an education in the power of signs and symbols, like learning about the meaning of a map in elementary school. The next day Fred would cut out the game story, including the box score, from the St. Louis Post Dispatch and attach it to the program, which contained the scorecard. Now the depiction was complete, in words and symbols, available for exploration and appreciation when excavating a memory, like a short story or a painting that evokes some distinctive imaginative and emotional response.

When I matured as a baseball fan, I came to appreciate a box score more than a completed scorecard. It is a game represented in miniature. Fred taught me the joy of studying a box score, the scholarly ability to re-create, in imagination, a game and the performance of players by understanding the information contained in a small space. I learned how to read it, what to look for, like a literature teacher shows students how to read a poem or an art history professor teaches how to look at a painting. A box score is a numerical marvel, but so much more. If read correctly it provides a narrative account of a drama as well as a quantitative depiction of a game. And it helps us to follow the stories of individual players as the season unfolds.

My love of box scores was another life-long gift I received from my father. That love became part of my satisfying morning ritual during the baseball season: wake-up caffeine and the pleasure of having enough time to study box scores printed in my daily newspaper.

My mother tolerated Fred's obsession with the Cardinals (and baseball) but didn't participate in it. For the most part she seemed indifferent to the outcome of games. As I grew older she may have thought it was pleasing that a daughter listened to and watched baseball games with her father. Yet at times I sensed a tension between them when it involved my father's attempt to turn me into a baseball-loving, ball-playing girl.

Jean, my mother, was plain, slight and small; dark haired like my father, but quiet and calm as opposed to Fred's big pulpit personality. She was bookish, a part-time librarian in whatever town we happened to live in as we moved according to the preacher's church assignments. She was active in the life and administrative tasks of the church: keeping the books, lining up special music for the services, scheduling the Sunday School teachers, making sure someone brought dessert for the covered-dish dinners. My parents wholeheartedly shared one overriding goal: to give their daughter an upbringing suffused with Christianity. Their relationship was a fairly typical mid-century modern marriage, like June and Ward Cleaver, or Ozzie and Harriet Nelson.

Jean wanted me to become a good housewife as well as a good Christian. She taught me how to cook, sew, wash, and iron. She had in her mind a clear notion of my future role, modeled on her own satisfying life. She couldn't understand the impractical instructions I received from my father, since no girl was ever going to become a baseball player, and she had no knowledge of any successful female athletes in any sport at the time.

I also sensed there was some sort of biblical imperative that informed her view of proper and traditional female roles in life. But I'm pretty sure she misunderstood Fred's desires. You see, his intention wasn't to turn me into a baseball player or world-class athlete. He just wanted someone to play with. He couldn't get the games out of his life.

Early in my childhood he recognized that I loved to run and jump, and that I had excellent hand-eye coordination. He bought a rubber baseball for me and encouraged me to play games when I tossed it against the house or garage. Before I played with a real baseball he bought a plastic ball and bat so he could teach me to hit, to play wiffle ball. My first glove was ordered from a Sears and Roebuck catalogue when I was eight years old – more serious instruction began.

A distinctive aspect of his attempt to teach me to throw a baseball correctly was his puzzling claim that the key was to avoid "throwing like a girl." But I was a girl; how did that make sense?

Well, girls usually tuck their elbow into their side when they throw. That's wrong. The elbow should be at the level of the shoulder when throwing a baseball correctly – overhand, not sidearm. "Get on top." "Grip the ball across the seams, for good carry." Jean looked on, mystified. Fred was encouraging but demanding. He could see I was beginning to throw "like a boy," but it was hard for me to do things right.

He said, "Baseball requires specific skills. You need to master the fundamentals first. How to throw. How to catch. How to set up when you hit." One day my lesson in playing catch turned to pain.

We were playing catch with a real, hard baseball, on the large lawn in front of our house. My mom was sitting on the porch steps, watching the to-and-fro, impressed with my improvement.

"She's comin' along," Fred says. Jean smiles. "But she's got a bad habit. When I throw the ball above her waist she's fine, because she always points the fingers of the glove up. But she can't catch a low ball cuz she hasn't figured out how to turn her glove over. You gotta point those fingers down to the ground. You haven't figured that out, have you Lizzie?" He looks at me. He motions. Fingers and thumbs up, hands together for a high ball. Fingers and thumbs down for a low ball.

He throws a few low balls, pretty hard. The first two go past me, then I club a couple. He throws a ball at my knees. I'm slow turning the glove over; it plunks me on my forearm, just above my wrist. Pain! Redness. A little blood. Well-defined seam marks on my skin. Lots of tears. My mom rushes to me, now lying on the ground holding my arm.

Fred says, "She's got to learn. You can't play baseball unless you can catch the low ball."

Jean yells (very rare): "Fred, let her be a girl!"

Fred walks to me. He looks down as I attempt to keep from sobbing. He's going to say he's sorry.

"Don't rub it, Lizzie."

Don't rub it? Is he serious?

"You're going to get hit when you play ball. It happens. So you have to shake it off. Be tough. Don't whine." Old school.

Jean stares at Fred, helps me up, takes me into the house, and puts ice on my arm.

What would happen now if a father plunked his daughter with a low fastball? He might be reported to Social Services for child abuse. Then? Fred was preparing me for sports and life. He was also trying to teach me a lesson about equal treatment. He saw no reason to treat me differently because I was a little girl. "Don't rub it" – straight from the unwritten rules of baseball, applicable to anyone who played the game, male or female, boy or girl.

Fred also made sure there was a basketball hoop available when I became old enough and strong enough to shoot the ball into the basket. He loved shooting baskets more than I did, at least at first. He put a backboard and hoop on a detached garage.

He constructed a pole, backboard, and hoop, with the help of members of the congregation, in a church parking lot, supposedly for the church's children. But it was really for us, father and daughter.

He taught me to shoot with good form, to put backspin on the ball, to release it high, with good arc on the shot. He created drills so I could practice dribbling. He taught me hooks and scoops and off-hand dexterity. We played hours of H-O-R-S-E and mismatched games of one-on-one.

And after basketball, if he had time, we passed the smaller-than-regulation-size football, ran patterns, and played a punting game.

Fred was a kid, and a coach, and a friend. He wanted a boy, but he got me. I was pleased to fill in. But there was also Pastor Fred in my childhood, a much different figure for me.

Whereas the Cardinal games were soaked in beer, my childhood was soaked in religion. It was there, every day, structuring my life, as real for me as anything I could see with my eyes or hear or smell. Christianity was in the air, a pervasive unquestioned and unseen presence to be breathed deeply, held and cherished, an atmosphere that formed a hazy bubble encircling our lives, an omnipresent background against which the foreground of everyday life was lived. But this background descended from the heavens on the other side of the world. It was here, but religion came from out there, as surely as light comes from our fierce burning star. It insulated our lives, keeping us safe from the melancholy of contingency. We were sure there was a Plan and we were part of it.

After all, I was a preacher's kid, so this is the way things should appear to me, isn't it? But this fact about me, being preacher Fred's daughter, didn't fully explain the way religion saturated my life. We lived in small towns, at least until my father was assigned to a church in Oklahoma City as I entered junior high school. In these parts of rural America, in the 1950s, first in Missouri, then in Oklahoma, a person's social definition had more to do with a brand of Christianity – Baptist, Lutheran, Church of Christ, Nazarene, Presbyterian, a few outliers called Catholics – than with a person's job or career. Social selves were religious selves; secondarily they were farmers, teachers, homemakers, insurance salesmen, or hired hands.

Everyone belonged to a church; people were somewhere holy on Sunday mornings and Wednesday evenings. Children were busy in early summer when vacation Bible school taught them to sing and play and to do arts and crafts in the loving arms of Jesus. For young people in our church Sunday nights were preserved for MYF: Methodist Youth Fellowship.

Children were aware of their membership in a distinctive and special tribe. I recall having my first theological discussion with a classmate of mine, a second or third grader, like me. I'm unsure how our discussion turned to religious matters. He told me that I would go to hell because I was a Methodist rather than a Baptist. My classmate was sure that only Baptists – Southern Baptists – could go to heaven. This bothered me a great deal. Being a preacher's kid led me to believe I was well situated to get the Big Reward if I played by the rules. Later my father assured me that Methodists and Baptists were on the same team. Although Methodists understood God's plan better than Baptists, as long as we put our trust in Jesus we would be saved – and Baptists loved Jesus, too. Our methods were different and better and more true, but Baptists were Christians. Pastor Fred's views about Christians were inclusive, ecumenical and communal, at least to a little girl who had never met a Jew, Muslim, Buddhist, or – God help us – an atheist.

I prayed every day, morning and night. "Now I lay me down to sleep…" I prayed for others less fortunate. I prayed for strangers. I prayed for the sick. I prayed before each meal. I memorized Bible verses. There were images of Jesus throughout our home, usually a parsonage next to the church. Our house was often literally in the shadows of a church and a large rooftop cross, overlooking our family.

Our life was oriented toward the most religious day of the week. Sunday School began at 9:45. We gathered and sang our first song: "9:45, 9:45, be on time for Sunday School at 9:45." This was an attempt to develop our character: punctuality is a Christian virtue. We read a Bible verse and talked about it. We did an art project related to the verse. Cutting and pasting, followed by a song – the song of my elementary Sunday school days:

Jesus loves me this I know
For the Bible tells me so;
Little ones to him belong,
We are weak but he is strong.

Yes, Jesus loves me
Yes, Jesus loves me

Yes, Jesus loves me
The Bible tells me so.

The ditty plays in my brain, immediately present in my memories as impressions, sounds that are as alive for me, even now, as the voices I heard coming from our radio as we listened to a Cardinals game.

At 11:00 the front doors of the church were closed. Stragglers could come in a side door in the back of the sanctuary without disturbing the service. Each Sunday I was there with my mother, seated in the second row, on my father's extreme right. He was elevated, on stage, behind the pulpit, moving, directing, singing, shouting. We Methodists loved music. Hymns and special music inspired us. The choir lifted the congregation, preparing us for the preacher's onslaught.

The service was tightly scripted, with little change week to week. The predictability was reassuring; in church we wanted no novelty. We sang familiar songs and professed together. The heart of our faith was expressed in the Apostles Creed, which we recited each service. As Fred looked down on the congregation, the pressure was enormous to fill the collection plate during the offering. After the sermon we sang the Doxology. The Altar Call was both an invitation and an ending – it rarely succeeded.

Later in life I was struck by how strange it was to be a preacher's kid listening to her father, experiencing his job, his career, his Calling – what he did with his life – much more directly than other children could know about their father's work. Fred's pastoral activities were varied, but the marrying and burying, the hospital visits, and the counseling sessions were not as immediate, for me, as the Sunday sermons. In his sermonizing I encountered the other Fred, the scary side of my father.

When we played sports together he could be demanding, but his behavior was usually consistent with the nice man I knew as my father. He never yelled at me or became too angry. He was kind and concerned and sensitive. On Sundays, however, up there behind the pulpit, he was another man. I admired him hovering over us, an impersonal spiritual leader more than a father. I respected him, but the underlying message of his sermons had more to do with fear than love. In Sunday School I was taught that Jesus loved me and we were all part of a family. In church the central point was messy; the clientele were taught to be wary, vigilant, aware of the menacing character of an individual human life – togetherness gave way to worry about our particular destiny.

Fred's demeanor during sermons was agitated, energetic, and angry. He didn't smile. He yelled. He pleaded. He warned. His concern was more threatening than reassuring. On Sundays he stepped into a role and played it aggressively, like a coach who, when he talks and acts, is playing a well-known character: the Coach. My father embodied another character, the Preacher, at least, as he understood the way it was defined by the expectations of his flock.

I asked one of my Baptist friends what her preacher was like. Does he yell? Is he nicer than Fred? Does he smile? Do you like him?

"He's scary. Yea, he yells a lot. Every Sunday. 'You're all going to Hell!'"

She added, "When I leave the service I don't feel so good."

As far as I could tell, Fred's message was fairly simple. In childhood, what later became complicated was uncomplicated. Metaphors were not really metaphorical; religious language was literal. God lived in the sky, in a place called Heaven. Our goal was to get there, to be with God forever. Unfortunately people were very bad. I found this puzzling. Most people I knew were nice and kind. They smiled and seemed happy. But deep down, I was told, they were swamped in sin. This was the central point that Fred tried to bring home.

"SIN!" I can hear Fred shout the word. The "s" was loud and long; it hissed like a snake, a serpent that harasses our equanimity and leads us into the abyss, estranged from God. If we let our sinful nature guide us we were destined for Hell, a literal place, very hot and miserable, with all manner of awful, terrible things that would happen to us – forever. Very disturbing for a little girl.

But there was hope. God sent his son Jesus to save us from our sins. If we opened our hearts to Jesus Christ we would be forgiven. The only way to get to Heaven and avoid Hell was to trust in Jesus, to have faith in Him. He would wash away our sins. God loves us, but if we do not do as he says, if we do not live as he wishes, he will send us away forever.

I tried very hard. I went home, shut my bedroom door, and prayed to Jesus. I talked to him: please come into my life. There were times when I felt warm after I prayed. Light. Calm. Joyous. A sense of relief. I was having a religious experience while still in elementary school. I repented my sins, although I wasn't quite sure what I was repenting. I treated people well. I didn't say bad words, as some of my friends did.

Once, as I left the house to play catch with my father, my mother asked me if I had finished my homework. "Yes," I said, although I hadn't finished my arithmetic problems.

Guilt. Shame. How could I have done such a thing? I was convinced I was going to Hell. After I prayed I felt much better because Jesus forgave me.

The Jesuits have a saying: "Give me the child for the first seven years and I'll give you the man." Well, the Jesuitical maxim proved more effective in matters involving civil religion than Fred's sin-soaked story about the Fall of Man. His secular indoctrination worked – I learned to love the Cardinals and worship in stadiums whose sacred spaces offered more meaning for me than the pews in a Methodist church. It was baseball more than hymns and professing – and Pastor Fred's preacherly performances – that connected my early life and later life. It wasn't my Jesus-infused soul that I carried into late life; it was my deteriorating body that had once been alive with the ecstasies of play. All of those prayers fell flat – and I wonder how that happened. That's the story I want to tell.

When I was old enough to play organized sports I found out I was good. Playing with my father developed my skills, but God, I thought at the time, had given me the ability to take advantage of divinely inspired coaching.

Each year in grade school we celebrated spring by taking an afternoon off, away from the classroom, for Track and Field Day. Little boys and girls competed against each other – separated by sex, of course – for ribbons: blue, red, yellow, and a white one for participating. Everyone received a ribbon! In sixth grade I won four first place ribbons: a dash, the standing broad jump, the high jump, and the softball throw. I could run faster, jump higher, and throw farther than any girl in my school – and I could beat most of the boys.

Our school sponsored a fifth and sixth grade team for girls in basketball and softball. We played other grade schools in nearby small towns. In basketball, in the degraded six-on-six form played by fragile girls at the time, I was a forward (not a guard). I was a phenom – dribbling, shooting, scoring, stealing.

Softball was a problem for me because…it wasn't baseball. The ball was too large and difficult to throw. When I made good contact at the plate the ball sounded like a dull thud when it hit the bat. I wanted to hear a sharp crack, as in baseball. I wanted to play on the boys' baseball team but teachers and the principal feared for my safety. I played shortstop. I was the best hitter. Fred said I made more plays than Marty Marion.

My father came to all my games. He radiated parental pride. People said, "She plays like a boy." Jean was afraid I would get hurt. She wasn't quite sure that sports were proper for girls. She may have thought that when puberty kicked in I would come to my senses and act more like a young lady. She was wrong.

| two |

Conway, Oklahoma

In the summer of 1962, the year I entered seventh grade, we moved to Oklahoma City, an attractive jolt after our itinerant life in small towns as Pastor Fred moved from church to church. My parents assured me this pastoral assignment would be semi-permanent, at least until after I finished high school. Nomadic life had not been that difficult. I made friends easily but didn't think much about them after we moved. My parents thought that stability would be good for me as I reached high school. My father was excited by the prospects of being the spiritual CEO of a larger church.

The feel of life in a big city was like putting a car into a higher gear. Everything was faster, more exciting and energetic. People were busy, involved, constantly on the move – more cars, busy streets, stoplights rather than stop signs, neon dazzle, impressive shiny high rises, the solemn pomp of the State Capital, a downtown where people swarmed like packs of animals, thrilling amusement parks, a go-cart track near us, and unlimited possibilities for shopping – unlike the small town squares where we had been limited to J.C. Penny, Ben Franklin, T.G.&Y,

and a Rexall drugstore. Penn Square Mall opened in 1960, a fabulous collection of stores, including John A. Brown, a department store with an escalator, where I bought my first books: Nancy Drew, the Hardy Boys, and Chip Hilton. We had moved to the center of things, away from the periphery. We caught up with the twentieth century.

We lived on Northwest 43rd Street, a few blocks west of May Avenue, a main thoroughfare for buying and selling – a street alive with streams of cars and trucks, a tunnel of energy and commercial life. I thought the busy-ness was great, but Fred and Jean often complained about the city sizzle. Soon they had modified their intentions; they longed for a return to a less complicated, more pacific way of life. Two years later we were headed back to Tiny Town, USA.

Instead of a parsonage, we lived in a 1950s brick ranch-style house, a few blocks from Pastor Fred's new church. Our house looked like all the other ones in the neighborhood, identical brick exteriors with similar floor plans: a small living room, two (or three) bedrooms down the hall, one bathroom, hardwood floors, an eat-in kitchen tucked into the back of the house, a small yard – clean and simple, just enough space to keep Jean busy when she wasn't involved in activities at the preacher's workplace.

The rhythm of our life still revolved around the church. My father's sermons were as pointed and aggressive as usual, but the audience was larger. Now there were more opportunities for his Altar Call to be successful. Maybe there was more sin in the city – or born-again successes were a function of packed pews.

The best part of our new church, for me, wasn't really a part of the church. In the back there was a small gymnasium built on the main building, not large enough for adult games of five-on-five basketball but useful space for youth practices and games, and pot luck suppers, or for kids to play while their parents attended to the workings of the church during the week. The gym was also ideal for solitary hours of shooting by a single girl. If members of the congregation walked past the door of the gym and heard the thump-thump of the basketball and the squeak of a single pair of sneakers they assumed it "must be Lizzie" shooting hoops by herself. There were shootarounds with the pastor and games of one-on-one when a basketball-obsessed girl could find a partner.

The surface of the court was tile rather than hardwood – probably cheaper and more resilient. There were white, square, wooden backboards, orange rims, and delicate netting. If a high-arching shot swished perfectly, without touching the rim, the net would snap like the end of a whip, loop under the basket, and wrap itself around the iron. A net-wrapped rim was a sign of a perfect shot.

I loved everything about city life: friends, school, teachers, basketball and softball teams, movies, shopping, energy – and my own personal gym. I looked forward to attending Northwest Classen, south on May Avenue, the best high school in Oklahoma City.

One day in early summer after my eighth grade year, my father knocked and came into my bedroom.

He looked very, very serious. Someone died?

"What's up?"

"I have somethin' to tell you, Lizzie. I have a chance to move to a small church in northwest Oklahoma. I've talked with your mother – and I prayed very hard. I think the Good Lord has other plans for me – for us. I can feel the spirit of the Lord guidin' me, Lizzie. I want you to pray about this, too. I think the Lord wants us in another place."

I was stunned and angry, tearful. I told Pastor Fred I wanted to stay. Why can't we stay here? I don't understand why we have to move again.

"Sometimes we don't know why the Lord intends things for us. But we must have faith to do His will. Everything happens for a reason, according to his Plan."

This was not an argument I was going to win. As usual, Fred had the Lord on his side. I prayed, as my father requested. I was old enough to wonder why I didn't get the response that Fred expected.

"Have you been prayin', Lizzie?"

"Yes, Father."

"Have you heard what the Lord wants you to do?"

"Well, kind of. But I'm not sure."

"Lizzie, you must keep prayin' and open your heart to the Lord."

"Yes, Father."

This kind of scene was one of many in my childhood, in which my father, Pastor Fred, was sure the Lord was speaking to him. I was asked to tune into the conversation, listen, wait to hear a majestic voice, and then assure my other terrestrial partner that I heard exactly what he had heard. But it just didn't work that way for me. Here I was, putting my trust in Pastor Fred, certain that he was in touch with the Lord, but unable to establish a good connection for myself. And in this case my anger and frustration about leaving Oklahoma City caused me to ask questions. How was Pastor Fred hearing what I didn't or couldn't hear? Is he really hearing God talk to him? I didn't know whether I should direct my anger toward my daddy or my Heavenly Father. My junior high despair was worthless.

Within six weeks we were packed and headed up Northwest Expressway, past Wedgewood Village Amusement Park, on the way to Conway, Oklahoma, population 1500 souls.

Why did we leave Oklahoma City? Fred and Jean were small town people, so they didn't take kindly to the commotion, the traffic, the impersonality of life in the city. My father wanted more. He wanted to be recognized as "Pastor Fred" by people at the grocery store or bank. He reveled in the role, the respect he elicited as a Man of God, a spiritual leader saving people from sin. In the city he was anonymous; in a small town, he was the Preacher, a character with transcendent status in the community. But there were other aspects of city life that bothered him.

There was a small park near our house, with a basketball hoop and an asphalt court, much more convenient than the church gym. I could slip out the door, dribble my outdoor basketball down the street, and be shooting baskets within five minutes. In the park my social world expanded; I made my first Black friend.

Georgia came to the park once a week. Her mother cleaned house for an elderly lady in the neighborhood, late afternoons after school, and insisted that Georgia not be left alone at home. My new friend was outgoing, upbeat, and very athletic. Tall and slender, with dark skin and an inviting toothy smile. She brought her own basketball. I could shoot better than Georgia, but when we played games she was quick and strong, competitive yet playful and genial. She told me she had never seen a "white girl" play basketball as well as I could. I was the only girl who could dribble around her and get to the basket.

At home I talked about my new friend but never mentioned that she was Black. As we were playing in the park one day I noticed Fred's car parked across the street, watching us. How long had he been there? I waved, but he didn't get out of the car. I wanted him to meet Georgia but he drove away.

"Who was that?"

"My dad."

"Why didn't he come over and say hi?"

"I don't know. Probably busy – had to go to church."

There were no Black kids in my school, nor were there Black faces in our congregation. There had been Black people in the small places where we had lived, but their houses were in different parts of town and they shopped in different stores and ate at their own diners. Segregated life had seemed natural, without friction or controversy – or so it seemed to a child. My parents approved of social life structured by a separation of white and Black people.

Shortly after Pastor Fred saw me playing basketball with Georgia he instructed me not to play with her. Since she came to the park on the same day each week, I was not to go to the park that day. I could play basketball at the church.

I asked my father why I was not to play with my new friend.

"It's against God's will," he said. "The Good Lord ordained the separation of the races. I will be preachin' about it on Sunday. I believe that God created the races and placed them on separate continents; he intended them not to mix. It's what the Bible says in Genesis and Leviticus, and in the teachings of the Gospels about Jews and Gentiles. As Governor Ross Barnett of Mississippi said, 'The Good Lord was the original segregationist.'"

I didn't understand why I couldn't be friends with Georgia. I talked to mother. I asked questions. I couldn't really talk to my father because his Biblical appeals and conversations with God always settled things – at least in his mind.

I overheard a kitchen conversation between Fred and Jean.

"Fred, your daughter has questions. That Lizzie, she's a thinker."

"Well, there are times when thinkin' can get you in trouble. A person can think too much. Instead of thinking she needs to be prayin' and readin' the Bible and havin' faith in the Lord to guide her. She's been taught that from the beginnin'."

"But it's natural to ask questions, Fred."

"No, it ain't natural. She needs to have faith. Thinkin' is the Devil's work. Thinkin' leads to sin. She needs Jesus, not a bunch of malarkey cloudin' her brain. You'll see. Best thing for her right now is to get away from this wicked city. Sin is everywhere – like Sodom and Gomorrah. Best we leave."

I think those two years in Oklahoma City gave my father a new sense of the changes that were inevitable but would take years to arrive, even in a big city, far from his small-town, backward white Christianity. In 1958 Clara Luper had led her Black Douglass High School students to downtown Oklahoma City to

Katz Drug Store, for the nation's first sit-in. They wanted to be served at an all-white lunch counter. Fred thought he could escape social change in the far reaches of northwest Oklahoma. And he was also protecting me from influences that would be absent as we found ourselves fleeing toward innocence.

We left for Conway on a hot day in early August, our car packed with clothes, kitchen essentials, books, and my sports gear. The parsonage in Conway would be furnished. Some members of the congregation were there to see us off and wish us well – final prayers and a few "praise the Lord's." The Good Lord would be with us.

This moving day was different. I was older and more attached to the place we were leaving. My prayers were becoming less successful, more uncertain. It was a day that left me with clear but indeterminate impressions – which may seem to be a psychological contradiction, but the fact is, I clearly didn't know what to feel. My trust in father and the Lord was swirling around in my head with questions about what I was giving up and what were the real reasons we were leaving Oklahoma City. Fred and Jean were excited and optimistic, with Christian smiles and expressions of faith in the "Good Lord" to head us further west. I didn't want to leave but there was again some unseen presence in the background pushing us away from something and toward something else. There was disappointment mixed with the pleasures of anticipation. Moving day was like going on extended vacation with a one-way ticket. I would never return to Oklahoma City until I could go alone. I tried to put my questions in the background and let Pastor Fred's faith – and his version of Christianity – guide us back to small town life. Conway might be good for me.

Jesus and the Cardinals were at the center of my early childhood. They were there as photographs in an old album, but without much emotional content to turn them into more than dead snapshots. As a child we take pictures, but there's something missing that brings an image alive, to make it appear as part of us – because we are not yet a self. We don't know how to react or make judgments about what is given to us. We don't know how to feel. So, there was Jesus... and there were the Cardinals. How these facts about my past became elements in a larger story, or whether they were disconnected moments or featureless atoms or parts of a unified flow – these things remained unrealized. The day we drove toward our new life in Conway was the day I began to come into my own in some new way.

We drove from Oklahoma City through gently sloping hills, faded green, spotted with grazing cows, politely decorated with small ponds and groves of blackjack oak trees, creased by small tributaries shaded by cottonwoods and elms, lined with dirt roads headed toward tidy white farm houses and stoic red barns.

Before long we had escaped the pastoral softness of a landscape more southern and were driving through vast open flat spaces that levelled the earth and allowed us to see for miles and miles to the vanishing western horizon, across brown scorched fields in the late summer heat. Earlier, the fields had been organic, alive with yellowish, tawny movement as the stalks of mature wheat yielded to the will of eternal winds in an Oklahoma summer. Combines arrived. Harvest left the country with thirsty sections of bland tilled dirt, the re-birth of a greening new crop still a few weeks away when the seed wheat would find its new home as the season changed and the weather cooled.

The further we drove, the more we left greenness behind and my mood became more flat, brown, and dull, to match the depleted landscape. By the time we reached Conway I was sure my life was on a downhill trajectory and my future was hopeless.

I wish I could say Conway was a charming little town and my spirits lifted as we entered from the south, but there wasn't much there to charm me. A few more trees – but it was as bland and flat as the surrounding fields, except for the water tower and two dominating white grain elevators at opposite ends of town, monuments to the farms, farmers, and farming that kept the community healthy, if not thriving.

There was a three-block main street running through the center of town, lined with a few businesses that would attract their scattered customers on Saturday mornings, more stores than we expected in such a small town: grocery, bank, hardware, a drugstore with a soda fountain, others…and two pool halls, which Pastor Fred called "beer joints" or "dens of iniquity."

If folks wanted a more specialized or broader shopping experience they could drive to Alma, almost twenty miles away, the county seat, population 7,000, home of Great Plains State College and wise high school kids who looked down on small-town rubes who appeared from the sticks to take advantage of the richer cultural opportunities provided by a small college town. I would learn these things in my Conway years.

But I had a get-out-of-hicksville card I played whenever I met another high schooler in Alma.

"Where do you go to school?"

"Conway," I replied. "I moved from Oklahoma City."

"You lived in The City? Why'd you move here?"

"My dad's a preacher and he was assigned to the Methodist church in Conway."

"That must have been cool living in The City." (Oklahoma City was always referred to as "The City.")

I was resurrected in the eyes of Almatians – as I called them – from a know-nothing inhabitant of nowheresville to a with-it member of those who are in-the-know. Oklahoma City was the Source…WKY and KOMA radio stations and the Bands that played on Saturday nights in the Armory or the American Legion building, hosted by celebrity DJs whose voices promised excitement from far away.

We drove through downtown Conway, past a large community building, a lot containing farm equipment for sale, an aging two-story high school – which I would attend later in the month – a detached gymnasium with a rounded, curving roof, an elementary school, two tennis courts with basketball hoops, and a large playground. We turned left; in two blocks we pulled up to the Conway Methodist Church and a boxy parsonage with ugly pink siding, built by members of the congregation five years earlier – convenient for the preacher's family but uninspiring and architecturally plain. Welcome to my new home in Conway.

Fred's mood was upbeat; Jean looked serene. They could see I was unimpressed with our new home.

"Cheer up, Lizzie. The Good Lord knows best. Trust Him."

Jean added: "It's for the best, Lizzie. Just you wait and see. Give it a chance. It's where we belong."

I don't remember much about our first days in Conway, before school started. I think I had packed my journal and didn't find it until a few days later. There are no entries until late August, yet I do have a vivid memory of making my first friend.

Shortly after we had arrived, members of the congregation organized a meet-and-greet luncheon. The former pastor and his family, who had already moved on to another church, returned for "fellowship," as we Methodists called such things. A short program included some music from a member of the community. Did he belong to our church?

His name was Harry Berens, a gentle older man, well into his 70s – tall and gaunt, his cowboy shirt and jeans hanging from his bony frame like over-sized clothes dangling from an under-sized mannequin. He had multi-day white stubble on his face and a wispy, white comb-over.

He was well-known in the community, yet people hardly knew him. He often would appear at community events, uninvited, and offer to "sing a few songs and tell a few jokes," as he said. People could hardly turn him down, although they might suggest there was time for only "one or two songs," padded by brief introductions containing a couple of strained attempts at humor.

His guitar, whose body was deep brown and glossy, produced a rich, clear sound, big and round in lower ranges yet precise and crystalline when he picked the smaller strings. It was a 1936 Martin D-18 – he told me later – purchased during the depression when he took advantage, in a kindly way, of another person's desperate need for a few dollars.

His singing voice was on the shaky side of an aging Willie Nelson – not bad, but not so good. His guitar-playing was solid but unspectacular, mostly standard chords accompanying traditional, non-religious songs. He liked Hank Williams and Woody Guthrie, a program more appropriate for PTA meetings or the annual FFA stock show and luncheon than a get-together in the basement of the Methodist Church, Conway, Oklahoma.

After he ended the short program, no one stepped forward to thank him or to wish him well. He seemed lonely and shy – odd for someone who had just performed in public.

I walked toward him and introduced myself.

"Hi, Mr. Berens."

"Harry. Just Harry."

"Harry, my name is Lizzie Ware. My dad is the new preacher here. I really liked your songs and your guitar playing."

"Thank you so much, my dear. Lizzie. Is that short for Elizabeth?"

"Yes, it is."

"Do you mind if I call you Elizabeth? That was my late wife's name."

"No, I don't mind at all."

I complemented him on his beautiful guitar. He told me it was a very fine guitar and he had a story about it.

"It's a very special guitar, Elizabeth. Someday I'll tell you about it. Do you play?"

"No, I don't play guitar, but I'd like to learn."

"Well, Elizabeth, how would you like me to teach you to play guitar?"

"I'd like that very much."

And that was the beginning of a beautiful, short friendship with Harry, my septuagenarian best friend.

Harry owned a number of guitars, so I borrowed one, and with my parents' permission, began my lessons, once a week, usually in the church basement. Harry drove to Conway from his farm, a few miles from town, in a green 1952 Kaiser, one of a small fleet of Kaisers that he owned. Kaiser-mania was one of Harry's idiosyncrasies – which I never understood. He drove only Kaisers. He had accumulated them through the years, parked randomly around his farmhouse and outbuildings, some still usable, others just lifeless antiques available for parts and aesthetic appreciation. "Isn't it a beaut?" Harry gleamed. Black ones. Green ones. Some sleek older ones, more boxy. One smaller curiosity, a two-door coupe, was called a "Henry J," which had something to do with the parent company that built Kaisers.

Harry also was a rattlesnake hunter. For me, spring meant baseball. For him, spring was when rattlesnakes come out to sun themselves and provide opportunities for Harry and other crazed hunters to stalk and snag these reptiles with broomstick-like equipment, spring-loaded pinchers on the end, jury-rigged in shops like Harry's.

One day when I visited Harry on his farm, for my lesson, he greeted me with a mischievous smile.

"Elizabeth, I want to show you something."

He walked to the trunk of a Kaiser parked in the driveway by the back door of the farmhouse and raised the lid.

"Look here."

There in the trunk was a writhing, rattling, slithering, angry-looking mess of reptilian horror, unhappy about sharing a close space in a homemade screened box in the trunk of a car with other creatures who were also unfortunate victims of the Okeene Rattlesnake Hunt and Harry's odd interests.

In a short time I learned much from Harry – from his stories and his parsimonious Midwestern religion.

In the sultry days before the start of school I filled the hours shooting sweaty hoops in the August heat, after which I escaped into our new home for a cool-down. I see myself sitting in front of the swamp cooler in the living room, sweet iced tea in hand, the blast of damp air on my face, insulating me from heat and sound and anxious thoughts about the coming year. In early evening, after Fred's busy day doing churchy things, I drag him – or did he drag me? – outside into the heat, behind the church in an open ballpark-like grassy area, where we play catch and he hits fly balls to me. I pretend I'm Curt Flood chasing down a deep one on the warning track in Busch Stadium. We return to the moist coolness of the kitchen, where the radio sits on our dining table, ready for us to tune to the Cardinals – from KCRC in Enid, Oklahoma, or KMOX in St. Louis, the evening blow-torch that created the Redbird tribe throughout the Midwest and the South. Harry Caray and Jack Buck take me to the world of my imagination as Fred listens with me, pitch by pitch--and we hear the beer man in the crowd.

It had been a tough yet hopeful year for Cardinal fans in 1964. After starting slowly they had traded one of their best pitchers, Ernie Broglio, for an unknown young Cubs outfielder named Lou Brock, a speedy player with all-star potential. But trading an 18-game winner for a nobody seemed to us – Fred and Lizzie – to be a bad deal. As the summer progressed we began to change our minds. Brock was turning into a star for the Cardinals. They called up Mike Shannon from the minor leagues, another young outfielder with potential, and fired their general manager. But in late August the Cards still trailed the Philadelphia Phillies by over 10 games – stuck in fourth place. Fred gave up; I still had hope. During the last week of August our team won six straight games, but the Phillies still looked like the best club in the National League. September proved to be a magical month for the Cardinals and for me. It was the month the Cardinals would come from behind, the Phillies would collapse, and our Redbirds would win the National League Pennant. It was the month in which I would become friends with Jacob Tucker.

Jake was in all my classes, except Home Economics, in which I, along with other high school girls, learned how to become a high-functioning housewife. We learned how to do domestic tasks while the boys took a class called "Vocational Agriculture," in which they learned the fine arts required for being a farmer. As a whole, we were a group of future housewives and future farmers, members of organizations, Future Homemakers of America (FHA) and Future Farmers of America (FFA), that reinforced our assigned roles in life. Our education defined our futures.

It took only a few days at Conway High to understand social life in ninth grade; it took longer to have a sense of the players in the higher grades. I became the tenth member of the class, six boys and four girls. Although the girls and boys didn't talk much to each other or socialize in class or at lunch or in study hall, it was impossible not to notice Jake. He was outgoing – at least to the other boys, and he was everybody's friend. Big personality, big smile, over-sized laugh. Verbal, smart, opinionated – smartest kid in the class, at least until I arrived!

He was already the size of an average man, almost 5'9. The boy didn't grow much taller in high school although he lost a few pounds here, filled out there, and became stronger. Blue eyes, dirty-blond hair. His face was somewhat round, small chin, thick neck, square body, big biceps. I had him pegged as a catcher. He had an innocent, energetic, full-of-life presence that expressed rural good cheer and confidence, strength and self-assuredness. He was raw but mature, a boy-man, despite being only fourteen going on fifteen years-old. His father had died when he was younger. His early maturity may have been a function of more responsibilities on the farm where he lived with his mother, a mile from Conway. Yet his maturity was laced with an irresistible playfulness and bubbling sense of humor. He could put in a hard day of work on the farm but the party didn't start until Jake arrived. Work hard and play hard. Have fun, but stay out of jail – he had to be available the next day for the fields - baseball and wheat. He led, and many followed.

As I left school after one of the first few days of the semester I heard the unmistakable sounds of baseball: the ball hitting a bat, the chatter of players calling for the ball. *Ball! Ball! Mine! Mine!* I was attracted to a field not far from the high school building.

It was a beautiful little field, well-maintained, watered and edged and mowed to produce a natural work of art in which the splendor of the field would inspire the players to rise to the level of the pristine space in which they played. In my high school years, following our baseball team to tiny towns in northwest Oklahoma, I learned not to be surprised when we pulled up to an untarnished, self-contained little beauty, grass-dirt-grass (no unglamorous, uncivilized skinned infield), far away from big-time baseball, the field a sign of the love and care bestowed upon the game by country fans who knew that sometimes a prospect could be found on the backroads, amidst the wheat fields, if a scout drove far enough and dug deep enough – and all the boys deserved to play the best game in America.

I sat on the bleachers and watched a fine-tuned practice led by Mr. William Ross, "Coach Ross" to his players, "Coach Bill" to parents and fans, "Chief Bill" to sneering detractors who could not quite accept the fact that an "Indian" could lead their boys, and "Mr. Ross" to students at Conway Junior and Senior High Schools. To me he would be Mr. Ross, my physical education teacher that year; next year he would introduce me to Oklahoma history, seen from the perspective of a member of the Cherokee Nation, a distant relative of Chief John Ross, whose acquaintance I would make as Mr. Ross's students learned a historical story about our state that was untold or mis-told in our textbook. And he was "Coach Bill" when we began basketball practice later in the fall term. A man of many roles in Conway public schools: junior high social studies, physical education, high school Oklahoma history and civics, boys' baseball, girls' basketball, and gentle counselor to confused boys and girls.

Coach Ross was solidly built, over six feet tall, with skinny legs and a square torso – high cheek bones, attentive wide eyes, a keen-edge chin, like Kirk Douglas or Dudley Do-Right, the Canadian Mountie; bronze ancestral skin and intense black hair. His manner combined calmness and command; he coached with quiet authority. He moved with the grace of a former athlete and managed practice with conviction, honed by years of experience on the baseball field. He handled the fungo – the long, slender bat used to hit practice flies and grounders – with the style of an elegant artist whose instrument becomes one with his body. Backhand toss – the fungo worked as a seamless extension of his hands, arms, and shoulders, lifting well-placed fly balls to outfielders, slapping flawless, back-spinning two-hoppers to infielders to allow them to find the rhythm of the light-stepping, semi-circular approach to the ball – step through, with efficient momentum toward first base as the throw is made. I heard him say, "Rhythm through. Get through the ball."

Fred taught me to appreciate an infielder's dance, as well as an outfielder's straight-line path to the ball – no meandering, no drift or over-confidence that you can get to the right spot in a leisurely way by delaying your arrival until the exact moment the ball can be caught. In the outfield, to arrive early isn't bad manners; good fundamentals require early arrival. Tardiness doesn't allow for the possibility of misjudgment caused by the wind or the sun or an errant misreading of the swing or the sound of the hit – factors that can fool a player and misdirect the trip to the ball.

I watched from the weathered set of bleachers as Coach Ross instructed players in familiar fundamentals; Coach Fred, with the help of the Lord, had given me an introduction to the alchemy of the game. Yet these skills would remain dormant for me because Conway had no softball team – and I surely wouldn't be allowed to play baseball with the boys.

Why was there a baseball practice now, at the beginning of school as autumn approached, when high schools should be practicing football? Are they already practicing for the spring season?

In very small schools in Oklahoma, those too small to have a football team, there was a fall baseball season, with a short September schedule, playoffs, and the crowning of a state champion in October, after which boys – and girls – could start practicing basketball. At least I could watch baseball until our girls basketball team began practice.

My attention turned from Coach Ross to the players, most of whom I did not know, except for a few of the boys in my class, including Jake, taking grounders at shortstop. He was very good, the best infielder in the group despite being a freshman. He was stocky, with thick legs – scouts like middle infielders with skinny legs – but good feet. Be quick but don't hurry. He was kind of bouncy as he approached the ball. There was an older player in the infield whose arm was stronger, but Jake's hands were more clean and precise; his feet skipped effortlessly toward the ball, and his throws to first were accurate. When it was Jake's turn to hit during batting practice he took swings from both sides, a switch hitter with a stronger, more natural-looking swing from the right side, and a short left-handed swing – solid line drives and sharp grounders, but without much power. In the matched races from home to first at the end of practice his strides were short, quick and twitchy, rather than long and fluid, yet he was still one of the faster players.

I saw these things from the bleachers that first day, but I didn't see all of them, because I had to be taught to see with the eyes of a scout, then re-create them later in reflection on that first practice. Fred had introduced me to the art of watching a game, how to look for the finer details that produced a deeper appreciation of the excellences required for playing well. Later, Coach Ross, a bird-dog scout for the Yankees, helped me to advance beyond Baseball Appreciation 101. I couldn't play – but I could be taught to see.

After a few days of watching practice from the bleachers, Coach Ross walked over to me as practice ended.

"Hello there. You're Lizzie Ware, ninth grade PE, right?"

"Yes sir, Mr. Ross."

"I see you here almost every day. You like baseball?"

"Yes sir, Mr. Ross. I love baseball. My dad, Pastor Ware, taught me to play. We play catch and he hits me flies and grounders – and we listen to games on the radio and watch the Game of the Week on Saturdays."

"The Cardinals on the radio?"

"Yup. They're my favorite team. I love the Cardinals. How about you? Do you have a favorite team?"

"I do. The Yankees – but I like the Cardinals, too. Do you have a favorite player?"

"Stan Musial. I saw him play at Busch Stadium. I was sad when he retired. Do you have a favorite player?"

"Mickey Mantle. Did you know he's from Oklahoma?"

"No."

"Would you like to play catch?" A slight upturn of his lips.

"Sure. But I'd have to go home to get my glove."

"You don't need to do that. We have an extra glove and catcher's mitt in the bat bag."

So we played catch – but not at first. He began by tossing the ball softly, from a very short distance. I knew his arm was warm because he had just thrown batting practice. He didn't want to hurt or embarrass me. After a few throws his lobs began to annoy me.

"Mr. Ross, you don't have to be afraid you'll hurt me. Let's play catch. You don't have to treat me like a girl."

"Alright, Lizzie. Let's play catch."

As I warmed up, I stepped back to increase the distance between us. He threw harder. I played catch as an infielder. Throw overhand. Step to the ball. Move your feet. Hands together when catching. Find the seams. Extend the distance. Make your catch-and-throw less an act of leisure and more like a play in a game. At the end of the session we were playing long-toss, better to strengthen the arm.

Mr. Ross keeps my final throw and walks toward me, with a very big smile. He reaches out to shake my hand. "Lizzie, you've been taught well. Your fundamentals are better than most of the boys on the team. Your father taught you well. Did he play?"

"In high school and college, in Missouri."

He hands the ball to me. "Show me how you hold the ball."

I take the ball and place my index and middle fingers, slightly separated, lightly across the big seams, with my thumb underneath on a seam.

"Good. I notice your throws have good carry – no tail."

"You know what I hate worst about softball, Mr. Ross? The ball is too big. It's hard to throw. Girls have smaller hands. That makes no sense to me. And the ball just goes thud when you hit it. It's not as much fun as baseball."

"We'll do this again. Do you play other sports?"

"Basketball. I love basketball almost as much as baseball."

"Then I'll see you on the basketball court, won't I? I'm the girls' basketball coach."

"Yes sir, Mr. Ross. I can't wait. Playing's better than watching."

"It is indeed, Lizzie." His voice trailed off. "It surely is."

I think there was some nostalgia in his voice, but he said no more about his own playing days.

The next day at school, Jake walked over to me as I put books into my locker. He said he had seen me play catch with Coach Ross.

"You're really good."

"So are you."

He was shy and somewhat awkward – a boy-girl ninth grade thing.

"I'm Jake."

"I'm Lizzie." Where was this going? His friends were watching. I should help him out. I told him my dad was Pastor Ware and that he had taught me to play, to love baseball – and the Cardinals. "We listen to their games every night. I've been to Busch Stadium."

It was as natural for me to mention the Cardinals as it was for Pastor Ware to invoke Jesus when talking about his identity. "Hi, I'm Lizzie, and I'm a Cardinal's fan."

But it was luck (wasn't it?) that the Good Lord should pluck me away from the big city and set me down near another fevered fan of the Cards. The mention of the Cardinals set Jake off, changed his body language, altered the pitch and rhythm of his speech, and added exclamation points to the end of his sentences.

"Did you listen to the game last night? Who is your favorite player? Mine is Dick Groat. Brock is hitting over .340. Bill White needs to hit better. Boyer might be MVP. McCarver is a great catcher."

I responded with an insider's grasp of secret knowledge shared only with those whose faith was equally strong. Within minutes we were bound together in a partisan friendship, a two-member cult. As far as I could tell, Jake's passion for baseball and the Cardinals was unmatched among his friends. When he discovered someone whose similar passions were smoldering, well, it was a match--a match made in the firmament called Conway High School.

Each morning before school we compared notes on the previous night's game. Unlike Jake, I didn't always last the full nine innings. If the Cardinals were ahead I usually turned off the radio before ten o'clock. Jake was sleep-deprived if the games went into extra innings.

In late September the Phillies looked to be sure pennant-winners with only twelve games to play. But they lost seven straight games while the Cards went 6-1. In the next to the last weekend of the season the Cardinals met the Phillies in a critical three-game series. The Redbirds won all three. My journal tells me that Ray Sadecki, a young left-hander, beat the Phillies on September 29. The next day Curt Simmons beat the Phillies' best pitcher, future Hall of Famer Jim Bunning. The Phillies now had lost ten in a row.

Jake and I could hardly concentrate in school during the last week of the season. We couldn't believe the Cards could lose to the lowly Mets on the final weekend, but they did – twice. Meanwhile the Phillies played the Cincinnati Reds, who were tied with St. Louis on the final day of the season. The Phillies were a game back. Philadelphia beat Cincinnati while the Cardinals beat the Mets. Our Redbirds won the National League pennant, the "Phillies Phold" was one of the worst late season failures in the history of baseball and I had a new best friend who just happened to be a boy. We were united by the ecstatic moment in which Harry Caray shouted from the radio: "The Cardinals win the pennant! The Cardinals win the pennant!"

In the World Series the Cardinals played the mighty Yankees, Jake's other favorite team. Mickey Mantle. Yogi Berra. Whitey Ford. Roger Maris. All were in the later stages of their careers. The weekday afternoon games were almost over by the time I walked home from school. I watched the weekend games, televised in ghostly black and white. The radio and TV announcers exchanged places throughout the series: my beloved Harry Caray, Curt Gowdy, Joe Garagiola, and Phil Rizzuto. The Series was decided in game seven, with Bob Gibson pitching against a young Yankees righthander, Mel Stottlemyre. The Cardinals scored three runs in both the bottom of the fourth and fifth innings; the Yankees came back with a three run homer by Mickey Mantle in the top of the seventh, his third homerun in the series. Ken Boyer hit a homer in the bottom of the seventh to put the Cards ahead 7-3. A Clete Boyer homer. A Phil Linz homer. Could Gibson finish? Bobby Richardson, who had thirteen hits in the Series, popped up to end the game. The Cardinals were World Champions!

There was only one teacher who indulged my requests to listen to game seven in class: Mr. Ross. I took our table radio to school, where it remained in my locker until our afternoon physical education class in the gymnasium. Mr. Ross placed it on the scorer's table, plugged it in, turned it up, and listened to Garagiola and Rizzuto do play-by-play as other girls shot baskets, largely ignoring what was going on in St. Louis at Busch Stadium.

After Mickey Mantle hit his homerun, Mr. Ross, who had been listening closely, turned to me.

"I played against Mickey."

"You played against Mickey Mantle?"

"I did."

"Would you tell me about it?"

"Some other time. Let's listen to the game."

Basketball practice began in late October after the baseball team had been eliminated in the playoffs. I was told that our girls' team had not been very good, and several solid players from the previous year had graduated. Ninth graders rarely played for the varsity, but Conway had a junior varsity only when there were enough girls to form a second team.

There were no "tryouts" because there were so few girls out for the team; we needed every body we could get. Everyone made the team, but that didn't mean every girl would get to play in the games.

Two other ninth grade girls played: Marcia Little, the town doctor's daughter, who lived in one of the largest houses in Conway, and Claudia Sternberger, the daughter of the richest farmer in the county – if rumors were true. They were best friends, cordial but cool to me. I was the new girl, the Preacher's kid, and a bit of a tomboy, at least by reputation after a few weeks in school. Any of these factors, along with my lower social status – the Preacher's income was small, his car was old, his house was plain, and his daughter was no fashion queen – might have been enough to chill the prospects of becoming closer friends with "The Rich Girls," as I called them. They formed a small insular group, which included a tenth grader, Diana McClure, the banker's daughter. The Rich Girls had nice clothes and an air of superiority. And they didn't quite know what to make of my baseball-filled conversations with Jake or my attendance at all the home baseball games. If my love of baseball and boyish behavior distanced me from the princesses, it was basketball that brought us together.

As practice began I hoped I could at least get playing time as a guard (not a forward) because I was quick and I could handle the ball – and I resolved to work harder than anyone on the team. A guard? Half a player?

In Oklahoma in 1964 girls' basketball was six-on-six, six players on each team. The game had evolved, now allowing unlimited dribbling and no center jump after each basket. Yet it was still a lesser version (in my mind) of boys' basketball. It seemed to have been created as a less strenuous modification of the boys' game – but it undoubtedly had its charms. The center line was an absolute marker separating two courts, each containing three forwards and three guards. Only forwards could shoot in their front court, with the opposing team's guards defending their backcourt. No player was allowed to cross the center line. Forwards played only offense; guards played only defense. If a shot was missed and a guard rebounded the ball, the object was to advance it to the frontcourt where it would be passed to a forward. While the ball was possessed in one half of the court, six girls would wait impatiently at center court until the action returned to their side. If a shot was made, one official retrieved the ball and threw it to the other official nearer midcourt, who handed it to a forward, standing in the small semi-circle inside the larger center jump circle, clock running. The forward would then pass the ball to another teammate, a forward, like any other in-bounds pass along the baseline or the sideline.

Girls' basketball was a continuous flow of two separate three-on-three games, one in each half of the court. The structure produced a more wide-open offensive game since there were only three players to run an offense, lots of space to maneuver, more difficult for the defense to clog the interior and double-team.

Mr. Ross became Coach Ross. I think he had studied the girls' game and he knew how to coach. We did all sorts of drills to develop our skills. We didn't scrimmage until the end of our first week of practice. Shooting. Dribbling. Passing. Running. He created competitions to evaluate our skills: free throw contests, dribbling races, around-the-horn shooting, agility tests. He matched us in groups, so we found ourselves cheering for our teammates. The Rich Girls were impressed.

"How did you get so good, Lizzie?"

"Lots of practice!"

They had more money and stuff, but I was a better basketball player. Now we had more in common: six-on-six became a social lubricant; my status was re-arranged, defined upward, while their status was defined in a downward trajectory on the court.

I found a new love. Bigger towns and cities had Friday Night Lights. In Conway and other tiny towns in northwest Oklahoma we had a Friday Night Gathering that brought the community together throughout late autumn and the winter months, until the days warmed and the landscape became more green, until the scents and sounds of spring arrived with the southern breezes. Girls' game at six o'clock; boys' game at eight.

By the second half of the girls' game the bleachers were usually full. The smell of popcorn filled the gym; the heavy atmosphere was flush with bodies packed together cheering for their kids – reconnecting with friends and relatives, feeling part of a far-flung community bound together on Friday nights by the play of their younger members. And I, too, began to feel that I had become a part of my new community – much more than on Sunday mornings when I listened with other Conwayites to Pastor Fred haranguing us about our sinful nature and our need for Jesus Christ to forgive our sins. When I walked downtown or went into a store it was common to be greeted by a stranger in bib overalls or an unknown overweight lady in a rayon shift telling me I had played a good game the previous Friday night.

I wasn't quite the star of the team, but I was one of the two best players. Our best player was a strapping farm girl, Mary Kay Snell, champion barrel racer in junior rodeo, a six foot source of sinewy energy who drove a tractor, put up hay, took care of her sheep and pigs – and set the toughest screens that were ever seen in Class C girls' basketball. Coach Ross taught us the finer points of the pick-and-roll, back screens, and motion three-on-three basketball. By midseason Mary Kay and I had become an efficient combination of strength and quickness. Big Mary Kay and Lizzie; she banged bodies; I drove around them. She posted strongly or rolled to the basket – I passed her the ball. I passed, she scored – they double-teamed her, I swished the net.

It was the most fun I had ever experienced playing sports. We surprised everyone by winning our district tournament, before losing to an eventual state semi-finalist in the regionals. Fred and Jean reminded me that the Good Lord knows best. We were meant to be in Conway, not Oklahoma City. At first I was devastated, but now I had to agree with my parents. The Good Lord must have been concerned about my basketball career, a Conway emerging star instead of toiling on the ninth-grade team at Northwest Classen, a mega-school in the big city. Medium-sized fish, very small pond.

Next spring Coach Ross asked Pastor Fred to become Coach Ware, to help with practice when his pastoral duties allowed – first base coach for games. And me? I was asked to be the Bat Girl. But I didn't find that demeaning. Coach Ross gave me a uniform. My new role allowed me to sit in the dugout with the coaches and players, listen to the brain-trust talk about the game, consider strategy, evaluate the action – even offer a little advice if I thought the coaches might have missed something. I usually sat with Coach Ware between innings and kept score. Coach Ross called me Coach Lizzie; he took time to explain things to me, to allow me to see with more experienced eyes. And I could talk to my best friend Jake during the games, as well as shag balls during batting practice and warm up as if I was one of the players. I wasn't quite a member of the team but I was surely more than a feminine mascot, less the object of condescension and more like someone who could know the game from the inside.

I loved the way Jake played baseball. He played hard; he was a hustler – first player on and off the field, at a near sprint. He ran out every ball, took the extra base, reacted quickly as a runner on a ball in the dirt; head-first slides, diving outstretched for grounders through the infield, best bunter on the team, seldom struck out. At the end of the game he wore the dirt from the baseball field. He played with passion and love of the game.

One day I asked who taught him to play so hard and so well. A little league coach?

"My dad. He always said: if you can't play hard, don't play. And always respect the game. Play it the right way."

"Don't you ever get tired of running so hard on and off the field? You don't have to do that."

Jake smiled. "Joe DiMaggio once was asked how he was motivated to do his best every single game. Do you know what he said?"

"No."

"He said there was always a chance somebody in the stands was seeing him play for the first time and he wanted to show what kind of player he was. For me, there's a chance that a college coach or a scout is in the stands and will think I'm the kind of player he's looking for."

"Do you want to play pro ball?"

His eyes widened and he spoke with a quiet intensity. "More than anything."

There was some bonding going on. We were like two warm-blooded molecules coming together, sharing our baseball electrons – and maybe some further attraction might develop. At this point Jake and I shared our love of baseball, and his big personality was drawing me more closely into his orbit. It was easy to be best friends with him, with no complications, simple elements, and no benefits of a certain kind. We were still kids.

That summer between ninth and tenth grade I played softball on a recreation league team in Alma – a let-down after being around the real thing that spring. I had the sense that I wasn't being treated fairly because I was a girl; sports couldn't be as important for me as it was for boys. And I was beginning to become aware of what was going on in the world beyond the fields.

| three |

A New Family, Mickey Mantle, and Death

I was fifteen years old when I began tenth grade in 1965; sweet sixteen would arrive on December 7, a famous date, I found out. My journal indicates that I was becoming more aware of events in our trifling corner of the 1960s, people in our community, important happenings in the world, and the distinctiveness of sensory impressions.

My body was changing – no surprise there. I wasn't yet a young woman, but I was almost a young lady. Puberty didn't throw me for a loop, but I definitely felt different: more grown up, but only on the way. I wasn't totally confused, yet I was in between. I started my period way back in sixth grade, so long ago; good timing or good luck, because I had seen the fifth-grade film about what was happening. My mother had left me uninformed. I began to wear a bra in seventh grade, although I didn't really need one. I caved into peer pressure. Other girls made fun of those of us who were "flat," exposed before gym class in the locker room, a large open area that left our developing feminine egos flattened. I pestered Jean until she acquiesced and bought me a flimsy little trainer, with not much to train. By the time I reached my sixteenth birthday, finally, I had enough curvature to attest to my sex but my profile was unimpressive.

Overall, I was less than impressed with what I saw in the mirror. Short black hair, large gray-green eyes, nose a little too large, dark complexion – everything else was pretty average, except the part of me that made me a good athlete: long legs and arms, slender torso and a small butt, broad shoulders, large hands – for a young lady. I was almost as tall as Jake.

Marcia, the doctor's daughter, convinced me I could improve my appearance by wearing some makeup, which I had never done. My mother was also absent in this part of mother-daughter instruction. My parents rebelled at first but I assured them a little artificial touch-up on my eyes and lips wouldn't change my character, and it might improve my appearance. Marcia and I won the skirmish and Jean actually helped me at first – preacher's wife turned guarded cosmetologist. Earrings were Marcia's next recommendation. She thought I was "cute." I thought I was the unassuming girl on the back row of the team picture.

I was forced to be at least minimally aware of "current events" because of a regular weekly assignment given by my ninth grade social studies teacher, who required students to write a paragraph describing some event that had happened the previous week. We were assigned to cover different categories: local, state, and national politics; international events (disasters, tensions, conflicts, wars); business; popular culture; sports! I was a regular reader of The Sporting News (the "Bible of Baseball") and Sports Illustrated, publications that were delivered to our house; now I also read The Daily Oklahoman, watched the evening news on television, and listened to news on the kitchen radio.

However, if I wanted some explanation or context for what was reported I usually consulted my basketball coach rather than my social studies teacher. Mr. Ross became more like an older friend than a distanced teacher. I regularly dropped by his office to talk, often about sports, but also to ask questions. What is happening in Vietnam? Where is it? Why are we fighting there? Why are there anti-Vietnam war rallies? What is communism? What is the Civil Rights Act? Why are Black civil rights marchers being beaten by police in Alabama? Why were there riots in the Watts section of Los Angeles? Do you like rock music? Do you like the Beatles? What is a hippie? Why do they grow their hair long?

1965 caused me to ask questions about war and race, music and culture. None of these topics were in the purview of Pastor Fred and Jean. Sunday sermons took place in a religious bubble, unrelated to contemporary life and current affairs, except for Fred's single-minded concern for sin and redemption and Jesus Christ's boundless love for us, notwithstanding the infinite threat of an eternity in Hell if we ignored the central message.

Mr. Ross was patient and knowledgeable, a student of American history with a keen sense of perspective and a desire to understand both the details of the present and the broader sweep of history. Unlike my classmates (including my best friend, Jake Tucker), who were bored in Mr. Ross's class on Oklahoma history (in the fall term of our tenth grade year), I was fascinated by the story of our state, and disturbed by our nation's treatment of Native Americans, including Mr. Ross's tribe, the Cherokee Nation.

I began to notice people in Pastor Fred's church. There was a tall farmer, Duncan Miller, who usually helped with the offering. He accepted the collection plate from Fred and towered at the end of the pew as it was passed from person to person, with shiny cowboy boots, a string tie, and a suit coat oddly perched on his torso because he secured only the bottom button of his coat.

There were James and Mary Dickson, who lived in a shack down on the river. He had long, stringy unwashed hair and was said to be a kind of mathematical genius, with a graduate degree and no desire for material success. Mary was pleasant looking but had crooked, stained, decaying teeth. Their daughter Lana (who also had bad teeth) was an older girl at Conway High, well developed in areas where my development was still on the way, with a questionable reputation. The rumor was that they left the front door of their shack open so they could share their space with chickens and pigs.

There were the Turneys, who lived in a run-down house on the edge of Conway, adjacent to a wheat field. Wesley was a classmate of mine, uninterested in school, loud and obnoxious, with few friends and a shaky future, although he appeared to have some talent as a petty thief. He dropped out of school his senior year, joined the Marines, and was injured in Vietnam in 1969. His mother had one notable feature, which was pronounced when she sat next to us or we talked after the service; evidently she did not bathe regularly.

Our congregation was sorted into groups according to material success and social status, suitably connected, with those occupying the lower group subject to nasty micro-hostilities: comments, looks, expressions, tone of voice, rumors, and other behaviors insinuated into the pattern of Christian smiles and welcoming arms that hid the condescending judgments of those who lived in the higher reaches of Conway hauteur. Pastor Fred was unaware that his church was providing me with a different kind of education than the one he intended.

Another teacher, a recent graduate of Great Plains State College, taught English my first two years of high school. Miss Turner opened the sensory world to me. She was small, plain, mousy. Quiet, and shy, she was ill-suited to making a living standing in front of boisterous farm boys and girls more interested in the obsessions of adolescence: appearance, the opposite sex, status, things. Large thick glasses, clunky matronly shoes, drab dresses, no make-up. After months in her classroom I decided she was a poet, not a teacher. No wonder she lasted only two years. My classmates made fun of her, especially when we covered units on poetry. Only when she read and talked about poems did she seem to wake up from a stupor of timidity and unconcern. She was moved by expressions of emotions more mature than we were capable of experiencing: love of nature, sensitivity to refined relationships, the puzzles of memory, the mysteries of self-identity.

Her task was futile. She wanted us to do something of which we were incapable: to become aware of bits of experience and to express that awareness in language less common than the cliches of ordinary speech. She assigned small poetic creative writing tasks that my friends thought were silly. These assignments soon changed the content of my journal.

I recorded impressions: the sounds of an approaching thunderstorm on the plains; hailstones hammering our roof like rubber mallets; weirdly vibrating windows as a bitter cold front came charging from the north; cicadas conversing on a close summer evening; birds demanding recognition on an opulent spring morning. My timid guide was teaching me to be more mindful.

I became more aware of the changing seasons and extremes of the climate, not because of meteorological curiosity or scientific wonder, but because of how the world made me feel, changed my mood, redirected my sensibilities. I associated impressions with scenes and personal events – sounds and tastes and smells connected me to the past in direct and involuntary associations as I experimented with memory and became more mindful of the present.

I told stories about the people I met or encountered in downtown Conway or in church. Look at that aging fat man with the waffled out-sized strawberry nose, who sits on a bench every day in front of Roy's Uptown Pool Hall…dirty overalls, darkened work shirt arm pits, tattered boots with smelly toes peeking out from holes. Did he arrive in Conway to escape the FBI after robbing banks during the Depression? No, he played catcher for the Cardinals, a buddy of Rogers Hornsby.

One day in early autumn Jean drives me to my guitar lesson with Harry at his farm. She drops me at the house, up a long driveway, through a large yard; she will return in an hour after visiting a neighbor for coffee and gossip. Dog, short for "Dinkey Dog," greets us. Harry and I sit on the porch looking south toward a newly-planted field in which the seeds are beginning to sprout slender fragile spires that will turn into green clumps ready to face the unpredictable winter weather. Unpredictable and extreme? One of Harry's favorite weather factoids: On November 11 the all-time high temperature and low temperature in Oklahoma City occurred on the same day, the result of a vicious front that turned Indian summer (83 degrees) into an artic-like, frozen night (17 degrees) in a matter of a few hours. In a natural flash a delightful autumn day was transformed into a white-out blizzard. Welcome to the Great Plains, as Harry said.

There are fields surrounding the house and outbuildings: a shed in which two Minneapolis-Moline tractors are parked – one of Harry's tutorials educated me about the superiority of his tractors, why M & M's were better than John Deere or Case or any other machines on the market; a shop in which he tinkers and fixes and welds; a chicken house, a small "granary" (as Harry called it) in which seed wheat is stored; a detached garage providing protection for one of his Kaisers. The grounds are sheltered by large elm trees north and west of the house, planted to reduce blowing dirt, eroding topsoil caused by dustbowl-type winds. He has a large garden west of the windmill, still producing vegetables in advance of the first frost, which will arrive before long. I play the piece I have been practicing. We play and sing a couple of songs together; my repertoire is growing. In the last few minutes he introduces me to an unfamiliar piece, with new chords and changes. We have some time to chat before Jean returns. Harry seems more subdued this day. I've noticed he appears more slender, his cheeks more sunken, his face unnaturally pale. He has an air of ill health.

I was worried about Harry. In the spring he was in the hospital for a few days. When I visited him and asked how he was doing, he said, "I've got some pains, Elizabeth. But don't you worry. I'll be back on the farm before you know it." Our lessons became more intermittent.

There were times when he couldn't play guitar with me because of his arthritis. I knew how much this bothered Harry because he liked playing and working with his hands: fixing and welding, working on his tractors, implements, and the combine. He was also an artist, on good-hands days. He created unusual metal sculptures out of the buckets and piles of materials scattered around the grounds and in the shelterbelt: pipes, screws, bolts, nails, heaps of iron, steel, and aluminum – all kinds of superfluous stuff he regularly purchased at estate sales around the country and turned into pleasing abstract configurations. He was also an accomplished painter, better when representing Great Plains landscapes than people.

He picked up a cough that forced him to postpone one of my lessons, a bad sign, because I knew how much he enjoyed our sessions. He told me so. "Elizabeth, I am so pleased that we can get together and play." But I was most worried about his mental state. When I first met Harry he was full of energy and optimism. He seemed happy and full of "piss and vinegar" (sorry, Pastor Fred). He told bad jokes and loved puns. Now? His conversations were dominated by scattered reminiscing, comments about his life coming to an end, and the challenges of old age.

He was a lonely old man in a period of decline. I tried my best to turn our conversation into shades of light, despite his tendency to darken the narrative. Goods of the past were stained by Harry's overarching sense of loss and absence--and the impending reality of death.

"Tell me about your guitar. You never told me the story about it."

He smiled, brightened, and patted his beloved guitar. "It's a 1936 Martin D-18, one of the finest guitars ever made. Worth a lot more money now than when I bought it from a guy from Tennessee named Johnnie Freeman. We used to hire extra help every summer during harvest, to drive a truck, cut wheat, then work the fields after the grain was in the elevator. Johnnie showed up at harvest for three or four years. Didn't have much. He hitchhiked one year. Thought it was a great adventure to leave the Smokies and head west. Good worker. Handsome guy. He'd leave with a big check and usually kept going west to California. Rode the rails. In the winter he headed back to Tennessee, picked up some odd jobs, and wrote and played music on the radio and in honky-tonks. During harvest he slept downstairs in the basement. At the end of a hot day of work we would get together, have a cold beer, and play songs on the porch, right where we're sitting. He played some of his own songs. I remember one he called 'I'm Gonna Dig Me a Hole in the Ground.' He loved to pick 'Wildwood Flower.' Elizabeth, he was so full of life. At the end of the summer I wanted to go with him, to head west on Route 66 – but I couldn't, of course. I loved my Elizabeth. I loved the farm too much to go off half-cocked. I loved Oklahoma – but I envied his freedom."

"So, what about the guitar?"

"Yes. The last year he worked for us he showed up with a Tennessee friend, Harrison Hamentree; we called him "Hump", not Harry. He was missing his right index finger from an accident. He was a baseball pitcher, semi-pro. He said his missing finger caused him to throw a natural curve. Big Cardinals fan."

"So am I! What about the guitar?"

"Johnnie brought this guitar with him the last year he worked for us. Very proud of it. Before he left he offered to sell it to me – really, to loan it to me. Instead of heading west Johnnie and Hump were driving back to Tennessee. Something had come up and he needed the money. Didn't really want to give up this beautiful instrument, but he said he'd be back the next summer and buy it back. It was sort of a pawnshop deal. I was happy to help Johnnie out and I'd get to play it for a year, so we had a deal."

"How much did you pay?"

"I could only spare a hundred dollars, but that was enough for Johnnie."

"He didn't come back?"

"That year was 1941, and you know what happened on December 7, 1941?"

"My birthday!"

"Is that right? Well, Johnnie joined the Navy after the Pearl Harbor attack. He wrote to tell me he'd see me and this guitar after the war. But I never heard from him again. I'm not sure what happened to him, or to Hump. I didn't know how to contact any of his friends or family. Johnnie never said much about anything back in Tennessee. And I never took a vacation to Maryville, his hometown, to look for Freemans. This old guitar has been my best friend since then – and it always reminds me of Johnnie and his footloose ways. Some day soon it'll have to find a new home."

I was sad that day when I left Harry's farm, as we drove back to Conway. The story about the Martin D-18 had a strange effect on me. It made me both happy and sad. I had never thought much about old age and death, or about the passage of time. Pastor Fred talked about Heaven and Hell each Sunday, but they were just words without content; they were nothing more than concepts to be filled by a child's imagination, without any connection to tangible elements in life. Deaths of relatives were more like rumors than real events. Pastor Fred did a lot of marrying and burying, but I never attended funerals.

I was filled with the sense that my good friend, my gentle, kind friend Harry, was going to die, and that I must do everything I could to make him happy in his final days.

I encouraged Harry to attend church. I wanted him to be with other people. He said he had tried Pastor Fred's church shortly after we moved to Conway.

"I tried, Elizabeth. I came late and sat in a back pew. I saw you sittin' up front with your mother, second row, on your father's right. I liked the music, but to be honest, I don't like to be preached at and I don't like to be yelled at. Nothin' personal, about your dad. I know preachers think they have to yell and spit and tell us we better shape up or we're going to Hell, but I just don't need it. I don't like to be told what to do or how to live."

Don't need it? Everybody needs it – that's what Pastor Fred had been preaching since I could remember first hearing him.

"Harry, have you been saved? Have you accepted Jesus Christ as your personal savior and asked Him to forgive your sins?"

Harry looked at me and then looked away, south, across the fields. He was silent for a few moments, gathering himself, wondering how much to say to an adolescent preacher's kid.

"Let me tell you another story, Elizabeth. Let me tell you about Charles DuPont from North Carolina."

I wasn't sure why we had moved from Jesus Christ to Charles DuPont.

"I fought in World War I, Elizabeth, and it changed me. I was in the Army, in the infantry in Europe. I saw some horrible things and I was forced to do some very bad things because I was a soldier. I saw many people die. Death and suffering were with us every day, all around. I prayed hard, but at one point I gave up hope. Most of us believed we were going to die and that our prayers were useless. Some of the strongest Christians were dead; I saw soldiers shot, blown up, and gassed.

"I got to know Charlie, a fine, courageous, thoughtful guy. Well-educated. He had studied literature at Duke University. He had a beautiful southern accent and a passionate way of expressing himself. He loved the poetry of the great American poet, Walt Whitman, *Leaves of Grass*, which he carried in his pack and sometimes read to me. Charlie was smart and better educated than I was, but we hit it off. I told him I painted; he was a poet. Maybe that brought us together. And he was fascinated that I grew up on a farm staked in the Cherokee Strip Land Run of 1893. He had a kind of a storybook, wild west view of Oklahoma – cowboys and Indians, big skies and open spaces – like Edna Ferber wrote about. He said he wanted to visit me after the war."

"Did he visit?"

"No, Lizzie, he didn't make it. You know, there's an old saying that there are no atheists in a foxhole. Do you know what that means?"

"No."

"It means that when you're in a situation in which you might die, in a foxhole, in war, a person will have to turn to God, for hope, for believing there's a Heaven he'll go to or that he will survive. Well, Elizabeth, I've been in a foxhole with Charlie DuPont and he didn't believe in God. He didn't disbelieve, but he would say, 'Harry, how the hell (sorry for my language) do I know whether there's a God? If he's there, he's a lot bigger than puny preachers make him out to be.' Charlie thought it didn't matter whether you believe in God. If God exists, He surely understands human weaknesses, since he created us. And He's supposed to love us. Charlie hated preachers who make people feel guilty and afraid."

I had never, ever, heard anyone talk about God in this way. "What happened to Charlie?"

"He was killed, Elizabeth. He was trying to help another soldier and was blown up by a grenade. He was the finest, smartest, most interesting man I ever met. I decided I didn't have to worry about Charlie goin' to Hell. That doesn't make any sense. Any God I could worship wouldn't send Charlie to Hell because he tried to think for himself. When I was sittin' in your father's church hearin' him shoutin' and pleadin', I was thinkin' about Charlie."

I didn't know what to say. "Harry, do you believe in God?" I had never met anyone who didn't believe in God.

"I don't know, Elizabeth. I'm not sure what I'm supposed to believe in. I don't understand God. I don't understand the story most preachers tell. And there are lots of stories and preachers in the world. I pretty much gave up thinkin' about religion a long time ago. I agree with Charlie. It doesn't matter what you believe."

"Don't you hope you'll go to Heaven?"

"The war taught me that you can be good without God – you don't need religion to do what's right – or to know what's right. And it taught me to love livin' – which I do. But we have to die, don't we? It's disappointing. If there's more, things will take care of themselves."

I hear Harry saying, in a calm and gentle voice: "You can be good without God." I believed in God, I had strong faith, and I was sure Jesus loved me. But I was also sure Jesus loved Harry, whose voice was a new voice, a different one – so unlike Pastor Fred's voice that filled our little sanctuary on Sundays. I began to wonder and to think about the story of Charlie DuPont.

That summer I began to take piano lessons with Vera Tucker, Jake's mother. They lived on a small farm one mile from Conway on a paved farm-to-market road. I could ride my bike to my lesson. My guitar lessons with Harry were less regular now because of his poor health. I loved music and I could practice on the church piano in the basement community room. A new music bond was formed.

Vera was a member of our congregation, one of Pastor Fred's most musical sheep. She sang in the choir and her big contralto ranged above others' voices when we joined in singing hymns.

She also substituted on the organ, although her best instrument was piano. She was pleased when I asked her about the possibility of piano lessons, which she had given for many years.

Big voice, big lady, big personality – stout, red-headed, energetic and gregarious. She was Jake's biggest fan, always in the stands for Conway's baseball and basketball games, head parent cheerleader, eyes closely focused on the performance of her son, quick to react to what she considered a bad call by an umpire or official, especially if a call affected Jake. She was loud and loving.

The Tucker's farmhouse acreage was smaller than Harry's but there was plenty of room for play. After my music lesson with Vera I met Jake outside where he might be shooting hoops on the basket his late father had attached to the side of their small barn, or he might be throwing a rubber ball against the chicken house, practicing his fielding. Our conversations at school were continuing; we talked about sports or exchanged stupid high school babble about classes, teachers, and classmates. We often sat together in study hall. But I had never visited his farm. Now I could combine a pleasant musical hour with Vera and an hour of play with Jake: shooting baskets, playing H-O-R-S-E, a skittish but scaled back game of one-on-one, playing catch, hitting grounders and flies to one another, throwing and kicking a football, and wiffle ball. An hour of play might turn into a longer ludic session as we played made-up games and competed as best friends, or as brother and sister, without the family drama. As far as I could tell he thought of me as a friend, a lover of sports, an agreeable companion who happened to be female – no hormones to complicate matters. At some point the invitations to come over after school or on a weekend were independent of a piano lesson with Vera, who became my number two (or three) biggest fan at basketball games. I was becoming a tiny-town star.

As our sophomore year progressed Jake and I did more and more things together: a Saturday outing to Alma with Vera, including cherry limeades at one of the drug stores with a soda fountain; a football game at Great Plains State College; a GPSC basketball game against one of the Oklahoma directional schools, Southwestern, located in Weatherford, down the road from Alma. We watched television together, usually sports: the Saturday baseball game of the week or the Sunday NFL game. Jake was a frontrunner fan; he rooted for the Green Bay Packers and the Boston Celtics.

We often studied together, doing homework and preparing for tests. He was probably a little better in math--geometry that year. He could sometimes see things more quickly than I could, especially when constructing proofs. I was his equal in biology and later in chemistry. But he had no interest in the subjects I found most fascinating: English, History, even Civics. Those were the classes that raised more questions for me; they gave me something to think about.

In Civics one day we were reading and discussing the Declaration of Independence. "We hold these truths to be self-evident, that all men are created equal, that they are endowed by their Creator with certain unalienable Rights, that among these are Life, Liberty, and the pursuit of Happiness."

I raised my hand: "I don't understand what a self-evident truth is. What's a self-evident truth?"

Mr. Ross: "What an interesting question. Let's consider some examples to try to understand what Jefferson is saying."

Later I wondered out loud: What could it mean for the Creator to "endow" men with rights? If He could endow them, could he un-endow them? And I wasn't sure what a right is. The class devolved into a conversation between Mr. Ross and me.

Jake didn't like my questions. "Why do you ask so many dumb questions?"

"They aren't dumb questions."

"Yes, they are. They're questions without any answers."

"How do you know they don't have answers? How can we even understand the Declaration of Independence without answering them?"

Jake couldn't see the point of asking my questions. I couldn't see how we could understand the Founding Fathers without asking and trying to answer these questions. Jake liked the precision of proofs and equations; I liked to think about big things. But our differences didn't prevent the bonds from thriving. I was beginning to feel other things about my best friend.

In the summer of 1965 the Kirchner family moved into the Miller farmhouse just a quarter mile down the road from Vera and Jake. Mr. Kirchner, John, had rented the house from Mr. and Mrs. Miller (who moved into Conway after a lifetime of living on their farm) and agreed to a sharecropping arrangement with the owners, including the use of farming equipment – a tractor, plow, spring tooth, one-way, and chisel – to work the land and make a living. The Kirchners populated the farm with animals: a milk cow, sheep, pigs, chickens, ducks, rabbits, two dogs – one indoor, the other a hardened outdoor stray who had come late to the family – and a group of cats whose lineage was uncertain. One hundred fifty-five acres of tillable soil and five acres of busy-ness inside the wall of trees that surrounded the house.

The children – Joshua, Ruth, and Sarah – were full-time laborers in a busy farm household, with assigned daily and weekly chores that left them little time (or so it seemed to me) to be kids. There were animals to be fed and watered, a cow to be milked, eggs to be gathered, a garden to weed, thirsty flowers, a barn to be cleaned, grass to be cut, a house to be dusted, meals to be cooked, dishes to be washed, clothes to be ironed...a well-disciplined family machine led by John and Virginia Kirchner.

I became acquainted with the Kirchners because I had volunteered to be a First New Friend (FNF) to Ruth, a year younger, a ninth grader in the fall term. Jake had volunteered to be Josh's FNF. We were ambassadors in a program established by Conway Methodist Church in conjunction with Conway Public Schools, whose goal was to lubricate the shock of the new for a family moving into a strange community – as well as to catch possible new recruits for Pastor Fred's kingdom. Our job was to welcome the new kids in the country – not on the block – to answer questions and make their first days in school and the community less difficult because they already had a...First New Friend!

At some point later in summer Pastor Fred and I left Conway for our first visitation...and recruitment. We called ahead to the Kirchners. We picked up Jake and drove to the Miller place, now the Kirchner farm, the family standing outside the house waiting to greet us, nicely aligned from father to mother to children, Papa Bear to Momma Bear to cubs, organized by an unseen photographer for the team picture in terms of height and age – but Josh's height messed up the naturally pleasing symmetry, the regularity of taller to shorter. He towered over the group. The introductions were made, we shook hands, and I looked up to Josh's smiling face.

"How tall are you?"

"Six feet two," Josh says.

Virginia adds, "And he's still growing. He really shot up last year."

My first thought – which, I found out later, I silently shared with Jake: I wonder whether he plays basketball. The Conway boys' basketball team had no starter over six feet tall. Josh could be the tallest transfer in the history of Conway sports.

John and Virginia offered to show Pastor Fred around the farm. They left us to chat awkwardly with Josh and Ruth, while little Sarah, nine years old, soon to be a fourth grader, played with the dog.

We asked Josh whether he played basketball.

"Just at recess, at school," he said. "I never played on a team. Dad doesn't believe in sports."

I was puzzled. "What do you mean, he doesn't believe in sports?"

Josh tried to explain. Later, I was able to fill in more details.

John (as well as Virginia) was a devout Christian, committed to follow, as closely as possible, the teachings of Jesus Christ. When it came to sports, John's Jesus differed dramatically from Pastor Fred's Jesus, who was, no doubt, a baseball fan. There is a passage in the Bible, in Philippians 2, in which Paul says this: "Do nothing out of rivalry or conceit, but in humility consider others as more important than yourselves. Everyone should look out…for the interests of others. Make your own attitude that of Christ Jesus."

I could see that John had a point. Sports are competitive activities in which my desire to win means that I want you, my opponent, to lose: I want to defeat you. Sports foster attitudes that are inimical to cooperation, humility, and concern for others. John thought that competitive activities produce pride and self-glory, but the only being who deserves glory is God. Jesus calls us to love others, to do unto others as we want done to ourselves, to treat others as we want to be treated. Josh's father believed that sports produce bad character; competition fails to love the other person, your opponent. So, John forbade his children to play sports or any games that involved competition.

When we first met Josh we didn't realize that his father's opposition to sports and competition was at the center of his understanding of the teachings of Jesus, while Pastor Fred's unsuccessful recruitment of John and Virginia was taking place. I was already plotting a tryout for our new recruit to Conway sports, not knowing my hopes were doomed.

I loved the Kirchners immediately. They were warm, outgoing, serious but relaxed; they exuded Christian and midwestern niceness. Josh embodied the humility that Jesus taught and John demanded. Ruth became the younger sister I never had, and Sarah provided the playful exuberance of a child for whom the world is a place of endless fascination and enthusiasm. Virginia always greeted me with a hug and a smile and unending, unfeigned questions about how my life was going, as if she was deeply interested in me.

Later Jake and I coordinated one of my piano lessons with an opportunity to work out our rookie. Since it was baseball season we started by playing catch. First problem: Josh was left-handed and we had only gloves for right-handed throwers. But Jake's old glove was loose and worn so Josh could put his thumb in the glove's little finger, his index finger in the first finger of the glove, and the rest of his hand in the glove's thumb. It became more linear, almost like a first baseman's mitt. So far so good.

Next, we showed him how to grip the baseball. Loose in the fingers, across the seams. "Have you ever thrown a baseball?"

"No, but I throw things all the time. Rocks. Gourds. Hedge apples." We began to toss the ball, Jake and I side-by-side, alternating throws to Josh.

His arm was long and loose; his whole body was long and loose. His legs seemed too long, disproportionate in relation to his torso. When he ran to retrieve the ball – it took some time for him to get comfortable catching with an ill-formed glove – and later when we threw a football and ran patterns, he ran with lithe, graceful movements, supple strides, effortless motions. He threw the baseball from a high three-quarter angle without any instruction. We corrected his flailing right arm and before long it was tucked and efficient.

When we changed to wiffle ball, he was rougher. He had to be shown how to hold the bat. Soon he was making consistent contact.

Next, we shot baskets. He had played some basketball on the playground, he said, at school, but his form was crude. We offered a few hints, to give him the notion that a proper release put backspin on the ball. His shot would be a work in progress. He eagerly took instruction.

While waiting his turn to shoot he exploded toward the basket, without the ball, as if he were imitating something he had seen. He took off and leaped, stretched his hand far above the rim, and landed softly, like a ballet dancer performing a choreographed move. Jake and I looked at each other, as if to say, "Did you see what I just saw?"

I walked to Josh, standing underneath the basket and handed him the ball. "Do you know what it means to dunk a basketball?"

Josh looked at me curiously. "No, not really."

I explained. "You run up to the basket, jump, get your hand high enough above the rim to throw down the ball, and jam it!" I performed the throw down with an empty hand. "You try." I handed him the ball.

He took only one step back from the basket, then one step forward, put his feet together, leaped, and jammed the ball down through the basket with two hands, as natural as a newborn baby taking to his mother's breast.

He grinned. "That's fun! Let me try it when I run toward the basket."

The first attempt failed because he lost the grip on the ball. His hands were large, with long, slender fingers. On the second attempt he palmed the ball shortly before takeoff, leaped too quickly, too far from the basket, I thought, and defied gravity by dunking the ball with a rim rattler.

We had discovered a gifted natural athlete who had never played a game of organized sports, who had never been taught or coached, whose inherent strength and athleticism had been improbably gestating on the farm, far from the fields and courts where his natural physical gifts could be turned into the useless skills that produce athletic achievement. Jake and I were giddy with the possibilities, but to no avail. Josh would be our hidden treasure, included in our play and games at Jake's farm, but unknown to the fans in the community and to the larger world. We asked and Josh's father answered. He was steadfast in his refusal to let Josh play sports. Henceforth he would be our teammate, our playmate, when we played our games on the farm--and our star football quarterback and wide receiver when we sneaked him into our Sunday touch football games behind the church. John never found out.

As we left the Kirchner's farm that day Jake and I were hopeful; Pastor Fred was disappointed. His recruitment failed.

"Are the Kirchners coming to our church?"

"No, Lizzie. They are members of a little church in Alma, the Church of Christ, Scientist. They are Christian Scientists."

I had never heard of Christian Scientists. I would learn more about the Kirchner's religion in the future.

In the fall term of my tenth-grade year I met a new teacher, although I had become acquainted with him in his other roles: gym teacher, girls basketball coach, and baseball coach. He was now Mr. Ross, Oklahoma History teacher, not to be confused with Coach Ross or the genial man I call "Coach" when I met him in the hallway or lunchroom, or I went to his office for an informal chat.

"Hi, Coach."

This man and his class had an unusual effect on me. I would soon be sixteen years old. I suppose I was typical in many ways, despite the two ruling passions that were always hovering in my life: Jesus Christ and the St. Louis Cardinals. My mother called me a thinker because I asked questions – which seemed natural to me. My relationship with Harry, who was dying, began to produce the first stirrings, uncomfortable thoughts about my faith. Mr. Ross's oblique influence was also significant.

He never directly instructed us to change our perspective on the history of our country. For other students in class, all nine of them, Oklahoma history was just a matter of names and dates: the "Five Civilized Tribes," the 1830 Indian Removal Act, the 1835 Treaty of New Echota, Stand Watie vs. Chief John Ross, the Trail of Tears, the 1866 Reconstruction treaties, the Dawes Act of 1887, the Unassigned Lands, the 1889 Land Run, the Cherokee Strip Land Run of 1893. But these names and dates were merely references that held a deeper meaning for those involved in the historical struggles that defined the story of Oklahoma.

Mr. Ross was trying to make us look at history, at the world, differently. Instead of thinking about history as an impersonal record of recorded events, he wanted us to see things from the perspective of those whose lives were being recorded. I began to see history as the conjunction of personal stories, every bit as interesting as the fictional narratives I loved in novels and sports stories. As a member of the Cherokee Nation, Mr. Ross was connected to Oklahoma history and the history of the nation in a novel way that he could convey to us – if we were open and willing to learn.

He understood our narrowness. He knew what we had learned from our own elders about the story of our nation. Yet we knew nothing about the Indian Nations, whose sovereignty was recognized after the Revolutionary War, and we knew nothing about his connection to the history of another nation. In fact, the notion that a tribe would constitute a "nation" seemed peculiar. We had been taught the usual story about American exceptionalism: "one nation under God." We are the greatest country in the world and American history is the story about the birth and development of our exceptional status. I had heard Pastor Fred preach about America as God's chosen place, the intended embodiment of Christian ideals and values. The history of Oklahoma, however, was not such a glorified story for Native Americans; it was a narrative of theft and loss, broken promises and cultural disrespect and decline.

We had a boring textbook called *Oklahoma History*, but we also had an authentic storyteller to provide more details and to make the tale come alive. The story Mr. Ross told us about the history of Oklahoma, especially in the nineteenth century, diverged from the one we read about in our text, in content, emphasis, and tone. It also diverged from the story I was vaguely aware of, the one that seeped into my awareness from my parents and the people in my community, including Harry. Theirs was a narrative about courageous pioneer men and women who had arrived in Oklahoma to find a new way of life, to acquire virgin soil, and to tame a wild land. There were people like David Payne, "Prince of Boomers," who led the charge into the Unassigned Lands, a hero to many, a usurper to the Indians. The popular origin story of Oklahoma contained two big events:

The Land Runs of 1889 and 1893. Harry's farmstead had been staked in the Cherokee Strip Land Run of 1893. For the Cherokees their Oklahoma origins were filled with misery.

I first noticed a subtle difference between teacher and text when we began to study the forced removal of the "Five Civilized Tribes" from their ancestral lands in the southeastern United States: the Choctaws, Chickasaws, Creeks, Seminoles, and Cherokees. Unlike our textbook, Mr. Ross never referred to these tribes as "civilized." They were simply the "Five Tribes." I asked about this. How were we to refer to them in class discussions and on our exams?

The reference to these tribes as "civilized," Mr. Ross explained, was demeaning to the Five Tribes as well as to other tribes. Historians referred to the "Five Civilized Tribes" to describe how these tribes responded to attempts to transform Indian life after the Revolutionary War and early in the nineteenth century; however, it was a term that expressed the cultural prejudices of white society and disdain for Indian culture.

The goal of American political leaders was to "civilize" the savage Indians, teach them to speak and act like whites, to Christianize them and to help with their assimilation into white society. But these "Five Tribes," as well as others, were already "civilized." They had their own languages, customs, rituals, religion, and forms of government. They had their own culture. They weren't savages in need of "civilization," as white society thought. They were culturally distinctive. When assimilation failed and white thirst for their land boiled over, removal by enticement became the strategy; land in what became Oklahoma was offered, and the story of Indian territory, with its sordid origins in a Land Grab, began.

My classmates grumbled about learning "Indian history" rather than Oklahoma history or American history. Mr. Ross taught me to appreciate complexity in places that others see more simply – in history and elsewhere. I was beginning to learn more broadly.

One day after Oklahoma History class I reminded Mr. Ross that he had never told me about playing against Mickey Mantle.

"Come by my office this afternoon and I'll tell you about Mickey."

I entered Coach Ross's small office in the gymnasium. "Hi Coach. Tell me about playing against Mickey Mantle."

"Well, Lizzie, I finally played against him in high school, when he was a senior and I was a junior. I had seen him play quite a few times before that game – first on his dad Mutt's Sunday team down in Spavinaw. He couldn't have been more than 13 or 14 years old, a little guy playing with grown men, mostly miners and farm laborers. I think he played second base that day. I remember two things about that game. First, he was a switch-hitter, and second, he was probably the fastest player on the field. Gosh, could he run!

"I grew up in Picher, which is a few miles north of Commerce, Mickey's hometown. I knew his wife Merlyn, who was also from Picher. Our school played Commerce in all sports. Both schools were in the old Lucky Seven Conference. I saw him play other sports besides baseball. An amazing athlete! He was good enough to be recruited by the great Bud Wilkinson to play football at OU, and in basketball he was one of the two big stars on the team – scored over 20 points in some games.

"It was in the spring of 1949 that I pitched against Mickey and the Commerce High baseball team. He was seventeen years old. Two years later he would be playing in Yankee stadium. Can you believe it? He wasn't as big as you might have imagined if you had never seen him play and you knew only that he had the reputation for hitting tape measure home runs. He wasn't even six feet tall. Maybe 5'10" or 5'11", about 175 pounds."

"Could you see that he was going to be great?"

"It's hard to say. He had plus physical tools. No one ran like he did. He had a strong arm. At that time he was playing short-stop, but I remember he had an erratic arm and made errors often. His power was just astonishing. People couldn't believe that such a small young man could hit a baseball so far. And the fact that he was a switch-hitter added to his potential. But this was small town baseball. Who knew that a kid playing in northeast-ern Oklahoma could play in the Big Leagues – and become one of the greatest baseball players of all time? Everyone now knows the story about how he became a switch hitter."

"I don't."

"Mutt, his dad, was just crazy about baseball. He was a pretty good player himself, on town teams and semi-pro teams in the Tri-State area. He named his first son after Mickey Cochrane, Hall of Fame catcher and later manager of the Philadelphia Ath-letics. Mutt's main goal in life was to make Mickey into a big league baseball player. He worked in a lead-zinc mine. After work, every day, he played ball with Mickey, along with Mutt's dad, Mickey's grandpa Charlie. Mickey was a natural right-handed hitter, but Mutt insisted that Mickey hit left-handed against his dad, who threw righty, and hit right-handed against Charlie, who threw lefty. They practiced every day until dark.

"I also saw Mickey play in Baxter Springs, Kansas, just across the border from Picher, up highway 69, then take a right for a few miles. The Baxter Springs Whiz Kids were coached by Barney Barnett, an ex-minor leaguer who knew everyone in the baseball scene in the area, including big league scouts. He recruited a sort of all-star team that played in a Ban Johnson League and traveled all over the Tri-State area to play the best teams. They even played minor league teams. Mickey was, maybe, fifteen when he started playing for the Whiz Kids. My guess is that scouts first saw him playing for Barney Barnett rather than Commerce High School."

"What position did you play?"

"I was left-handed, so I played first base, outfield, and pitcher. I was the starting pitcher that day, and I was scared. I had pitched well early in the season but I was surprised when my coach told me to warm up in the bullpen before the game. I had grown three inches in the previous year to about my present height, a little over six feet tall. I was throwing harder, had a pretty good curve, and was learning to throw a change-up. So there I was, 16 years old, throwing to Mickey Mantle, about a month before he graduated and signed with the Yankees."

"Did you get him out?"

"Lizzie, I did get him out – first time up. I remember that day as if it happened yesterday. A humid spring day. Warm. A little breeze from the south, blowing out to left. The feel of the wool uniform. The smell of infield grass that had been cut before the game. And this young man playing shortstop: light hair, some-what square, serious, playing with a passion of someone chosen to do just what he was doing and doing it better than anyone else we had ever seen. And that big, boyish grin after he did some-thing great. In his first at bat, with two strikes, I tried to sneak an inside fastball by him and he hit probably a 400 foot foul ball down the left field line. Then I threw him a change that he just got under – a flyball to center that seemed to touch the clouds. His second time up I didn't get so lucky. I got behind in the count and tried to put a fastball on the outside corner. I missed the corner and found the middle of the plate. Mickey hit one of the longest home runs in the history of the ballpark – at least that's what people told me."

"Did you finish the game?"

"I pitched to Mickey one more time. He hit a line drive dou-ble into the gap in left center, then I was taken out of the game. Last time up he hit another home run, left-handed off our right-handed reliever. Two homers and a double. But the other thing I remember was a play he made at shortstop on a flyball down the left field line, behind third base in foul territory. It looked like an impossible play to make but he ran it down, deep down the line with his back to the infield. No one but The Mick could have made that play. I couldn't believe his speed."

"Was he cocky because he was so good?"

"Not at all. He couldn't have been a more decent guy. When he hit a home run he hustled around the bases with his head down. When he was with the Yankees he said he didn't want to embarrass the pitcher after he hit a home run. He was like that in high school. You could tell he just loved to play baseball and didn't act like he was the biggest thing on earth. A really nice guy, although he could blow up some if he struck out."

"And he signed with the Yankees – when?"

"1949. Tom Greenwade was sitting in the bleachers that day I pitched against Commerce. Tom told me."

"Tom Greenwade?"

"Tom Greenwade was the Yankees scout who signed Mickey not long after he graduated. He was a former minor league player and manager. He still scouts for the Yankees. I know him fairly well."

"How did you get to know him?"

"I'll tell you in a minute. So the Yankees sign Mickey for a very small bonus – most say it was $1500 but it was really $1150, after a brief negotiation. A lot of people think that Tom took advantage of Mutt Mantle, but he was just doing his job. There were other bonus babies getting $25,000, $50,000. Did Mr. Greenwade really know that Mickey would become "Mickey Mantle," one of the Greats of all time? He says he knew Mickey would become great, from the first time he saw him play. But I'm not so sure. There were other scouts around who could have offered Mickey a big bonus, but no one else offered. The Yankees signed him for a little over $1000 and $140 a month and they sent him to the Class D Independence Yankees team, about an hour north of Commerce. My dad and I drove to Independence later that summer to see Mickey play, in a double-header, and to see whether he could hold his own in the K-O-M League: Kansas-Oklahoma-Missouri. Mickey was seventeen years old. He played in about 90 games and hit over .300, with a few home runs and twenty stolen bases.

"The next year the Yankees sent him to play for the Class C Joplin Miners in the Western Association. He tore it up. He was already the best player in the league as an eighteen year old. I memorized his stats: He hit .383 with 199 hits, 30 doubles, 12 triples, 26 homeruns – and 55 errors playing shortstop. He went to spring training in Phoenix, in 1951, with the Yankees, became an outfielder after a bunch of errors at shortstop, and was the talk of the camp. The Yankees had planned to send him back to the minors – no one made the leap from Class C to the Major Leagues, especially no one nineteen years old. But Mickey made the club – and the rest, they say, is history."

"So, how did you get to know Tom Greenwade?"

"That summer, in 1949, Barney Barnett asked me to play for the Baxter Springs Whiz Kids, primarily as a pitcher, but I also played some in the outfield. I was a pretty good hitter as well as a pitcher. By the next spring at Picher I was the hardest-throwing lefthander in the area – at least I thought so. I was going to play for the Whiz Kids that summer and wasn't quite sure what I would do in the fall – maybe go to Northeastern State College in Talequah and try to play baseball. In my first start for the Whiz Kids that summer I pitched a great game against a team from Chanute – twelve strikeouts and I had a couple of hits. After the game Tom Greenwade introduced himself to me and my dad and offered me a contract to play for the Independence Yankees: 500 bucks as a bonus and $120 a month. I followed Mickey to Independence and became a part of the Yankees farm system."

"Wow. You played minor league baseball. Did you make the majors?"

"No, I didn't, Lizzie. I pitched well enough in Independence to get a contract the next year to play for the Joplin Miners, just as Mickey did. But midway through the season I hurt my arm, first my shoulder, then my elbow. The Yankees sent me back to Class C Joplin in 1952. We had a great team, with three future big leaguers: Johnny Blanchard, Jerry Lumpe, and Norm Siebern."

"I have a Jerry Lumpe baseball card!"

"But I lost my velocity. I tried to be a crafty, soft-tossing lefty, but it was obvious to the Yankees that I could never make the big league team with my stuff. They didn't offer me a contract in 1953, but I got signed by the Ponca City Dodgers back in the Class D K-O-M league as a two-way player, pitcher-outfielder. It was fun, but after that summer I realized I needed to think about a career. There wasn't much money in the minor leagues. I had taken a few classes at Northeastern State College. I decided I wanted to stay around baseball, so I earned a degree and a teaching certificate – and here I am, at Conway, teaching and coaching baseball and basketball. And doing a little bird-dogging for Tom Greenwade and the Yankees."

"Bird-dogging?"

"I kept in touch with Tom Greenwade after he signed me. He checked up on me in Independence and Joplin. I think he had a soft spot for me. He's part Cherokee and signed me, a Cherokee kid. I saw him at a game in Talequah when I went back to college. We talked about a kid who was playing that day and I checked up on him later. I sent a brief report to Tom, Mr. Greenwade. He asked me to watch another kid play, and after awhile we kind of formalized our relationship."

"What's a bird-dog?"

"It's a scout who works part-time for a full-time scout who is assigned to evaluate players in a certain area. Tom is an area scout. His area is Oklahoma, Kansas, and Missouri. Sometimes I hear about a kid or see someone we play against who might be a prospect. I write a report and send it to Tom. Other times he sends me a name and asks me to take a look, to save him a trip. I have a scout ID card that gets me into games, and Tom provided a stopwatch. If the Yankees sign someone I've recommended or helped to evaluate, I get a small commission. It's fun and keeps me involved in professional baseball."

"Very cool."

"There's something else that keeps me going. Tom Greenwade is pretty famous among scouts. He signed the Mick. He found that jewel, that gem in a small town in Oklahoma, son of a miner who grew up poor, without indoor plumbing, and just wanted to be a ballplayer. Now Mickey Mantle is larger than life; he's "the Mick," one of the all-time greats. He'll be in the Hall of Fame. When I drive to a small town to see a game and watch a player, I always wonder whether there's another one out there, out in the bushes – maybe not Mickey Mantle, but someone who is really good, a player who no one knows about, who might develop into a Big Leaguer. It's like a treasure hunt. You have to be able to see, to really see, and to imagine what a boy might be like when he grows into a man, and hones his skills and develops those natural tools, like Mickey's speed and power, into something special. You have to see through the roughness, the poor fundamentals, the bad habits, the bad days, to the core, the essence, to the natural abilities that can be nourished, and polished, and made to shine."

"Could you teach me how to scout?"

"I could do that, Lizzie. I could do that."

I walked into the kitchen after school. Pastor Fred and Jean were seated at the table, talking, sipping their afternoon tea.

"I have some bad news, Lizzie." Pastor Fred was familiar with passing on bad news – a vocational requirement. "Harry Berens died."

My eyes began to water, there was a choking sensation in my throat, and my stomach seemed to constrict. I took a deep breath to keep from sobbing, but I was unsuccessful.

Jean stood up, reached out, and put her arms around me. My father was unmoved, a real professional. "We're so sorry."

I was unsurprised, but shocked; predictable death, impending death, isn't real death. Foreseen death is like the relation of theory to practice, an abstract understanding that lacks the emotional force of the real thing. I knew Harry was dying. He was hospitalized again in late fall. Our lessons had stopped. He said he wasn't up to it. I had visited him a few days before but he was not very talkative. He looked terrible. It didn't occur to me that I would never see him again.

My father's emotional unavailability may have had something to do with the circumstances surrounding Harry's death. He was found in his bedroom by a neighbor checking up on him. Doors closed, the smell of gas in the air as Harry's friend entered the house, overwhelming when he opened the bedroom door, the small gas heater inert; like Harry, who was sleeping peacefully, never to wake up. The heater was still leaking its deadly fumes. Bad luck or good fortune? An unexpected end to the final stage or a well-intended and untroubled result – a benign tinkering that alleviated the pain?

Rumors circulated. I could tell that Pastor Fred was suspicious. Given his view of human nature it was easier for him to think the worst of Harry and his unfortunate end. Like all of us, Harry was a sinner; his final act was profoundly sinful. Poor Harry. How unfortunate, people said. Another "S" word was on their minds, as well as Pastor Fred's. I wanted my grief to be pure, but it was undermined by suspicions that shouldn't have mattered, but somehow did make a difference in my post-mortem thoughts about Harry.

He left precise instructions that involved me. He was cremated. He wanted no funeral. On the first day of spring I was to invite a few of his friends to the farm. He provided a short list, including Opal Jones, his last live-in housekeeper, an arrangement that had scandalized the community. There was to be no preacher or priest invited to our informal ceremony. I was to retrieve the small wooden box that contained Harry's ashes, as well as the book that was placed beside it on a shelf. I was to walk into the field across from the farmhouse, with the other guests, into the verdant expanse of spring wheat, and read passages that Harry had marked in the well-worn book that I carried along with his ashes. I read from Charlie DuPont's copy of *Leaves of Grass*, by Walt Whitman. "Song of Myself:"

"I celebrate myself/ And what I assume you shall assume/ For every atom belonging to me as good belongs to you."

"No array of terms can say how much I am at peace about God/ and about death."

"And as to you death, and you bitter hug of mortality...it is idle/ to try to alarm me."

"I bequeath myself to the dirt to grow from the grass I love/ If you want me again look for me under your bootsoles."

I finished with the final lines from "Great Are the Myths:"

"Great is life...and real and mystical...wherever and whoever,/ Great is death...Sure as life holds all parts together, death/ holds all parts together;/ Sure as the stars return again after they merge in the light, death/ is great as life."

After the reading we took turns spreading his ashes. Our grief was mixed with the joy of Whitman's words and Harry's life and the warm southern breeze gently touching our faces – the friendly sun and the vast sky of the Great Plains and a field where Harry was now at home.

A few weeks later I received a call from an Alma attorney, Mr. Cunningham, executor of Harry's estate. He wondered whether we might meet in his office. I had been mentioned in Harry's will. Please bring a parent to co-sign some papers with you, he said. We met the following Saturday.

When Jean and I walked into Mr. Cunningham's office the first thing I noticed wasn't the shelves packed with law books or the impressive power desk or the spongy, expensive carpet. I noticed a familiar old guitar case standing in the corner. Mr.

Cunningham briefly described the contents of the will. Harry wanted me to know. Upon the sale of the land, two quarters, 320 acres, the executor was instructed to give a considerable amount to Great Plains College, for three purposes: to fund a full tuition scholarship each year for a graduating high school student in the area; to endow a chair in the English Department, to be called the Charles DuPont Chair in Whitman Studies; and to provide supplies and resources for enhancing programs in the Art Department. Harry left money to some local organizations: The Great Plains Historical Society, the Northwest Oklahoma Craftsmen, and the Borderline Theatre. He also left a large chunk of money to the American Cancer Society.

"Which leads us, finally, to you, Miss Ware." Mr. Cunningham arose from the desk, walked to the corner, picked up the guitar case, walked back, and handed it to me. I opened it and there was Harry's 1936 Martin D-18. I looked up as he opened a drawer and withdrew Charlie DuPont's copy of *Leaves of Grass*.

"He wanted you to have the guitar and the book. He thought they might someday mean something to you."

Tears. A smile. A memory of Harry's voice. "They do."

"One other thing, Miss Ware. Harry Berens left you twenty thousand dollars, to be placed in a bank account, accruing interest, until you reach eighteen years of age, the point at which you become the sole account holder. Congratulations. It's obvious that Harry thought a great deal of you."

A few days later Pastor Fred asked me to see him in his church office. "I have something to ask you, Elizabeth." Never a good sign when he called me Elizabeth. He looked away and was silent for a moment.

"Was Harry Berens saved? Did he accept Jesus Christ before he died?"

"I don't know, Father."

"Did he ever talk about his relationship with Christ? He didn't come to church. I didn't know him. And I'm afraid, Elizabeth, as you should be. I am afraid for his soul. And it's a hard lesson for you to learn."

I looked away. I looked at the cross on the wall. I looked at the image of Jesus on my father's desk. The thought came to me very clearly, for the first time. I was sure at that moment that God did not send Harry to Hell. I was sure that God did not send Charlie DuPont to Hell. And I was sure that God did not send Mr. Ross's Cherokee ancestors to Hell because they resisted Christian Missionaries' attempts to save them from eternal damnation.

Without a word I turned my back on Pastor Fred and walked back to the parsonage.

| four |

Walt Whitman, A Farm Girl, and Mrs. Wilson

For weeks and months after Harry died I changed my nightly rhythm. Homework. My Martin D-18. Walt Whitman. The Bible sitting on the nightstand next to my bed became a lonely, less friendly book. It still rested on top, but now it hid a book below. Each night before going to sleep I read from Charlie DuPont's copy of *Leaves of Grass*, first edition, scuffed and faded and smudged, the dirty green cover slightly warped, its spine missing an outside cloth. If the book was placed on a shelf with other books it was distinctive because of its anonymous matted spine, no title or author to identify the poetic fire within. On its inside covers Charlie had written notes about places and battles, a travel log of suffering and death. Now Charlie's book, then Harry's book, was my book. The passages I read at Harry's ceremony, in the wheat field, before the ashes floated down to dirt, were still highlighted. Whitman's words were Harry's words; they also acquainted me with a casualty of war, a man I never knew.

My nightly ritual changed when spring came and the Cardinal games lit up the radio stations in the Midwest and on the Great Plains. My transistor radio was a hand-sized black rectangular piece of magic that primed my imagination for naïve attempts to understand what Whitman was trying to tell me. For a time I conjured images of Bob Gibson flying off the mound to his left as he released a wicked slider, or Lou Brock stealing second base, arriving in a straight-ahead pop-up slide, ready to advance if the ball trickled into the outfield. Then I let my radio rest and reached for Charlie's dangerous book, hidden beneath the sacred text that pointed toward Pastor Fred's transcendent realm. I entered Whitman's charged, electrified world.

When I began my nightly soirees with the mad friend of my friends, I was merely curious. Harry wanted to tell me something about his life and death and his friendship with Charlie. He was daring me to experiment, like being dared to take a first sip from a can of Coors, or being handed one's first cigarette, an initial test of adulthood in high school, the challenge to inhale. I told a story to myself. Harry wanted me to inhale a different air. He knew the atmosphere in which I lived. He knew that Pastor Fred appeared in Whitman's lines. "Pleased with the earnest words of the sweating Methodist/preacher, or any preacher…looking seriously at the camp-/meeting," was Harry, like Whitman, pleased with the sweating Methodist preacher? But how could he be pleased?

After reading Whitman's poetry there was a time for reflection, before sleep came. I understood – I didn't understand. The words were sometimes like a flash of lightning coming through my window – then a thunderclap. I read the words silently, then read them again in a whisper, to a room where I was alone but connected; I felt Whitman's bond to an infinitely interesting world, full of bodies working and sweating, like a preacher, doing ordinary things made extraordinary by Whitman's attention and words and exclamations – his vigorous associations with the details of the world.

Whitman mentions God, but almost as an afterthought. Why think about God and another world when there is so much about this world that fills and excites the plenum of everyday experience? For Whitman the world is so rich and worthy of our regard that God is superfluous. Or was I supposed to see God everywhere?

Divine am I inside and out, and I make holy whatever I touch or/am touched from;/the scent of these arm-pits is aroma finer than prayer,/This head is more than churches or bibles or creeds.

Was Whitman holy?

The book seemed strangely spiritual to me, in a way I couldn't explain. It made me feel grateful, not because the world was a gift from God but because of its overflowing richness. Whitman wanted me to wake up to this life, to our life, to my life. I began to write down passages in my journal.

"In all people I see myself, none more and not one a barleycorn/less,/And the good or bad I say of myself I say of them."

"I exist as I am, that is enough,/If no other in the world be aware I sit content,/And if each and all be aware I sit content."

"I am the poet of the body,/I am the poet of the soul."

"I am the poet of the woman the same as the man,/And I say it is as great to be a woman as to be a man."

"That I eat and drink is spectacle enough for the great authors and/ schools,/A morning-glory at my window satisfies me more than the/ metaphysics of books."

Metaphysics?

It occurred to me one night that Whitman might be Satan. I had heard much about this tempting character, from Pastor Fred's sermons and stories. The devil is always around to lead us astray, away from God. Our questions – my questions – might be the voice of Satan trying to destroy our faith. But Whitman's voice was too honest, too spiritual, too real for me to think that he was just another polished flim-flam man leading me to sin. Whitman's voice was more god-like than the smarmy sweating threats we received from pulpits.

"My words are words of a questioning, and to indicate reality."

"The sky up there...yet here or next door or across the way,/The saints and sages in history...but you yourself?/Sermons and creeds and theology...but the human brain, and what is called reason, and what is called love, and what is/called life."

I'm sitting on the porch one evening, with Whitman and the Great Plains. I listen. Whitman whispers:

"Logic and sermons never convince,/The damp of the night drives deeper into my soul."

I carry my tattered cover on a morning walk to the edge of Conway, where rural life butts up against a collection of human souls called a town. I hear the nearby country conversations of animals: cows, chickens, and birds, as Whitman might hear them.

"I think I could turn and live awhile with the animals...they are/so placid and self-contained,/I stand and look at them sometimes half the day long./They do not sweat and whine about their conditions,/They do not lie awake in the dark and weep for their sins,/They do not make me sick discussing their duty to God,/Not one is dissatisfied...not one is demented with the mania of/owning things,/ Not one kneels to another nor to his kind that lived thousands of/years ago,/Not one is respectable or industrious over the whole earth."

Whitman, like Miss Turner (a poet and pretend teacher now out of work), wants us, wanted me, to experience the world as a permanent source of...spirituality? Heightened awareness? Sounds. Tastes. Touches. Smells. People. The kinesthetic feel of life. The unsavory, as well as the delightful--every man and woman whose life is worthy of celebration and whose occupation is humanly worthy.

"I tramp a perpetual journey,/My signs are a rain-proof coat and good shoes and a staff cut from/the woods;/No friend of mine takes

his ease in my chair,/I have no chair, nor church nor philosophy;/I lead no man to a dinner-table or library or exchange,/But each man and each woman of you I lead upon a/knoll,/My left hand hooks you round the waist,/My right hand points to landscapes of continents, and a plain/public road."

I was, at times, shocked when I read, but Whitman taught me not to be shocked by anything he said – and to feel enlarged, a glass being filled. Shock wasn't the voice of conscience, it was an overlay of culture and religion on experience essentially innocent. Why should we be shocked by having a body, by being a body, physically engaged in life?

"I have said that the soul is not more than the body,/And I have said that the body is not more than the soul,/And nothing, not God, is greater to one than one's-self is."

In death Harry and Charlie were telling me something, neither preaching nor pleading. Sing a few songs and tell a few jokes and listen to the poet.

"And I call to mankind, Be not curious about God,/For I who am curious about each am not curious about God,/No array of terms can say how much I am at peace about God/and about death."

When I put Whitman to sleep at night, I had no more reason to hide him beneath a different set of scriptures. Let him breathe, the better to help me to breathe. Charlie and Harry and Walt were teaching me to inhale the world, deeply.

After two years in Conway I rarely thought about what my life would have been like if we had stayed in Oklahoma City. Fred and Jean were right: Conway would be best for me. But they had no idea that small town life in the 1960s, in a farming community in the far reaches of northwest Oklahoma, would be less than optimal for raising a proper Christian daughter destined for marriage, motherhood, a life in Cardinals Nation, and a close relationship with Jesus Christ, her personal savior.

When we had lived in small towns, in Pastor Fred's early career as an itinerant preacher, it had not occurred to me to think of a place as anything more than a momentary stopping point on our way through my father's Christian deployments – a preacher's kid as a service brat. I had no home. I remembered the excitement of living in a big city, but Oklahoma City became more and more distant. Conway had become my home. My life was rooted and my surroundings were familiar. I identified with the possibilities provided to me in such a small, isolated part of the cosmos.

Whitman helped me to discern, to attend to the details of my inconsequential world. Everyone is from somewhere, and my somewhere could be as worthy as Whitman's somewhere. We had replaced the sizzle of the city with something more placid, with its own flow and shape. What Miss Turner had started, Whitman had taken up and pushed forward.

"I am the teacher of athletes,/He that by me spreads a wider breast than my own proves the/width of my own,/He most honors my style who learns under it to destroy the/teacher."

I am athlete and poet! I have a teacher and he loves my game!

"Upon the race-course, or enjoying pic-nics or jigs or a good game/ of base-ball."

My journal describes a Conway year – a Whitman year. In late summer there is a county fair in Alma. I walk through tropical barns, rich with the smell of animal dung, where sweating young future farmers and homemakers tend to their projects as industrial fans blow stifling air through cages and pens, with blue and red and white ribbons attached, symbols of hard work and achievement...and good luck. Beyond the barns, the carnival promenade is stuffed with people carrying snow cones and cotton candy, and carnies bellowing and belligerently demanding that we stop and spend, take a chance to win a stuffed animal or a TUPO: a totally useless plastic object. A minor league Ferris wheel and a tilt-a-whirl and a merry-go-round, music blaring, vertigo mixed with screams and laughter. Bright red and greens and yellows – Times Square on the Great Plains. In the background, on the horizon of the cacophony: the deep sounds of the rodeo announcer and the faint roar of the standing-room only crowd cheering for the barrel racers and riders and ropers.

Fall baseball games on fields with no fences, grass that runs from the backstop to forever – no love for the game here, no respectful pristine fields. Gappers roll freely between the outfielders, with nothing to stop the ball until the fence of a distant wheat field, which is no fence that matters for the game. Inside-the-park homeruns are misnomers, since there is no inside, only outside, except for the partial barriers along each foul line, pick-up trucks lined like a row of tanks ready for battle, horns honking when the home team scores or makes a great play.

There are stock shows at school, where the community gathers to see animals show off and friends eat a communal lunch and admire the husbandry of their young farmers. They watch as the judge silently circles a group of animals, like a predator stalking its prey, a thoughtful experienced judge. He sees like a baseball scout, a wise evaluator of talent. This judge looks like an overweight catcher with a white Stetson rather than a mask, his pearl-buttoned shirt plastered to his beer-expanded belly. He pokes and investigates; he re-positions the animals until he's sure his judgment is accurate. He leads the winners to the center, where they stand as agricultural Olympians might, receiving polite clapping from friends and family, the young owners standing satisfied with their animal friends.

There's homecoming in Alma each fall, when alumni from Great Plains State College and Alma High School return to remember and to root for their hometown football heroes and go to the Big Show at the college, and remark on the winners of the pageant. They return to enjoy the parade, the high school bands and floats and horses, and new tractors creeping around the town square. A few parading clowns toss candy toward the kids and adults crowding on the curbs, smiling and optimistic, who watch the uncoordinated band lines pass, and the fat kids carrying the sousaphones and tubas struggle to march in time.

The Queen and her court (disappointed princesses) sit on the backs of convertibles with signs on their doors identifying the chosen, announcing the winner, most popular and beautiful, all fake-smiling, offering the stiff, rotating insincere wave and the politicians trail in more convertibles, hoping to squeeze a few votes from the festive collage of marching and music and gaiety.

The winter brings basketball games, the Christmas play at church, the Holiday productions at school – a high school chorus and community sing-along, post-performance hot chocolate, and warmth in the season of cold.

There are assemblies at school, the gymnasium bleachers filled with K-12 excitement, glad to be missing class and to be entertained by traveling jugglers, singers, comedians, and trainers, who show up, unannounced to students, and surprise us. They are escapees from a circus, funded by some unknown government program trying to add zest to the education of culturally deprived farm kids, far from civilization.

Spring means the greening of the fields. The wheat fills out – a change of color as the heads shoot up to the sky, and the flatness becomes a sea of rolling, brilliant movement. The southern winds begin to advance their stimulating lukewarm purposes, bringing moisture from the gulf. Blackening skies. Churning clouds. The possibility of a violent hail-producing thunderstorm that can turn a beneficent crop into a disaster area. Nature can wreck the pocketbooks of farm families, as well as businesses in Conway and Alma that depend on the grainy gold of a good wheat crop. And the rotating clouds might also bring disaster in town, as it had to a once-thriving community not far from Conway, now nothing more than a collection of empty lots where businesses had stood before the tornado in the 1940s. Spring means hurried trips to the basement of the church next door, just in case a Big One hits, and prayers, and a reminder of why we were called the Conway Tornadoes.

In the summer of 1966 Jake and I became more than just best friends. We were sitting in a swing on the front porch of the pink parsonage in Conway. Pastor Fred and Jean were inside, watching black and white television fuzziness. It was a close, sticky evening; the preacher was winding down after another intense Sunday saving souls for Jesus Christ. The porch swing was small, just enough space for two bodies to sit comfortably touching each other, pretending to ignore how nice it was to feel the physical presence of a member of the opposite sex. We stop talking for a few moments and listen to the summer sounds: cicadas chattering, frogs' guttural rumblings, a lone dog barking in the distance, a night owl who-ing – not much traffic to disturb the peace each evening in Conway after harvest.

Jake turns to me. "I want you to be my girlfriend."

"What do you mean, 'girlfriend'? I'm your friend and I'm a girl." I knew what he meant, but I was playing coy. I felt like I was at the top of the Ferris wheel, waiting for the plunge.

"No, not like that. I mean like, '*boy*friend-girlfriend.' You know what I mean. We go on dates and do other stuff together."

"Other stuff?"

He turned away, seemed to be summoning some courage from deep inside, looked back at me, leaned over and kissed me. Neither one of us knew what to do with our hands.

It wasn't exactly my first kiss. In eighth grade, in Oklahoma City, I had kissed a boy for the first time – on a dare. But that didn't count. This was a *real* boyfriend-girlfriend kiss; the first of many.

It was probably inevitable, given how much time we spent together, how much we liked each other's company, and human biology. Hormones were firing, the mysteries of the opposite sex were exciting our sensibilities, and our otherwise innocent relationship was bearing pleasant fruit – which had been slow to ripen. We hadn't been fast movers. Our friends – and Vera, not Pastor Fred or Jean – were probably aware before we were of what might be going on or what might develop.

"Yes, I'd like to be your girlfriend."

The next day I went to Marcia's house and told her what had happened. Jake had just advanced from being my best boy *friend* to my *boy*friend.

"Last night Jake asked me to be his girlfriend and he kissed me."

"First time? He hadn't kissed you before? You guys are always together."

"No, we've just been good friends. I like him a lot."

"Do you love him?"

"I don't know. I don't think so, not yet. But it could happen."

"Did you like it? The kiss?"

"Yeah, I liked it."

"Did he put his tongue in your mouth?"

"No!"

"That's a French kiss. That's the next step." Marcia sounded experienced. She was dating a boy from Alma. I heard Alma boys were fast movers.

"Did he touch you anywhere?"

"No! He didn't know what to do with his hands."

"He didn't try to touch your boobs?"

"No!"

"If he tries to feel you up, what are you going to do?"

"Feel me up? What do you mean?"

"You know. Touch you in *secret* places."

"I don't know. I'm a preacher's kid. I don't want to get a bad reputation. If I let him, will he tell other boys?"

"Probably."

"Do you let your boyfriend touch your boobs?"

"Maybe. Just a little. Nothing inside of my blouse, just outside. If Jake takes you to the drive-in, he'll want some action."

"Action?"

"Action. Back row. Heavy breathing. Fog up the windshield. That kind of action."

"I'm not ready for that."

"Yeah, you are. You'll see.

Two or three weeks later Jake asked me out for a date, to the drive-in movie. He would drive Vera's car. Now playing: "The Good, the Bad, and the Ugly," with Clint Eastwood. Spaghetti western. Loud gunfights. Not too romantic.

I asked Pastor Fred and Jean for permission.

"He seems like such a nice young man," my mother said. They knew Jake from church and MYF.

"Be home right after the movie ends," instructed my father.

Marcia was wrong. We parked in a middle row – no heavy breathing, clear windshield, and a few more kisses and some innocent touching. We were heading in a pleasant direction, but that was as far as we were going.

I was a town kid, like the rich girls, Marcia and Diana, and a few of my other classmates whose fathers and mothers were the workforce for the few businesses that provided economic fiber in our tiny town. But farming culture was dominant, in conversations and commerce and community. Rural influences were inevitable. My new boyfriend Jake was a key co-conspirator in turning a Conway preacher's kid into a farm girl. Did he have bigger plans?

We advanced from high school conversations about the Cardinals and playing games in the Tucker backyard, to the serious business of Conway socialization: hunting and fishing and farming. Jake taught me to shoot a gun. We chose from his assortment of firearms, first a .22 rifle, a gift from Santa Claus at a time in his life when most city boys Jake's age might have been hoping for a toy, not an instrument of death. My tutorials began with target practice, shooting discarded cans lined up on fence posts or aiming at random objects in the landscape. Vera thought our shooting was charming.

After a few sessions we went looking for big game in the shelterbelt, the windbreak surrounding the Tucker's homestead. Jake was gleeful when I shot my first furry object, an unsuspecting squirrel who remained lodged in a tree, bleeding and motionless, a head shot by an amateur sniper. My reaction wasn't what Jake had hoped for. He saw a piece of game; I saw a form of life with a nervous system. Now? I am horrified. My enculturation was unsuccessful. Then? I didn't quit. I became a novice rabbit-killer.

I graduated to a small shotgun. Jake called it a "4-10," better for hunting various kinds of birds: quail, pheasant, and doves. We tromped through wild grasses and weeds in a winding pasture bordering the creek that ran through the Tucker property. Teenage Tarzan and Jane. Jake wanted me to try his 12-guage shotgun, better for scattered coverage of a killing field, but after one attempt, which left me with a bruised shoulder, I decided to stick with the small stuff.

When the creek ran high in spring and summer we fished the mighty brown waters of Mule Creek. We drove to lonely ponds in hidden places, known only to people like Jake, who knew the secret homes of mudcat and carp and perch. Fishing stayed with me, despite my acknowledgement that there are nerve endings in the mouths of fish.

Vera tutored me in the fine arts of gardening, picking, and canning. The Wares had small gardens along the way, but nothing like the Tucker's half acre of abundance: tomatoes, corn, beans, peas, potatoes, and onions. The vining plants: squash, cucumbers, watermelons, and pumpkins, produced green tentacles that covered far-flung sections of the garden. In the riotous greenness of bushes and vines there was both order and chaos. The plants were put down in a calm, rational plan; then they did what they wanted, aggressively and randomly, humans be damned. There were daily demands: watering and weeding – no days off for absent leisure. After the heat of a summer day, the laborers carried buckets to the garden as the sun declined toward the tops of the trees to the west, the garden now shaded. We stepped carefully through the confusion of growth and plucked prizes from the plants, some of the crop fit for the county fair in August.

When the weather cooled, after a piano lesson we drove to the river to pick sand plums. We visited a neighbor's yard for bushels of pears, followed by the rituals of canning: the large pot of boiling water, mason jars, rings and seals, hot fruit and sugar, and rows of sweet delights to be stored in the cellar.

It was up to Jake to turn me into something more than a gardener, canner, or cook. I helped the Tuckers gather eggs from their chickens – the Wares were chicken-less – and Jake's sheep also required daily attention. (If I was there for play I might as well get acquainted with the sheep.) But there was something else I wanted. There was a clear division of labor among farmers when it came to working the fields, planting the crops, and harvesting the wheat. For the most part, men did the field work and women were the support staff. I didn't see why women couldn't do what men did. It seemed to me like the differences in baseball and softball.

Jake taught me to drive a tractor. After his father had died, Vera hired a trusted friend to do the farming and to further the instruction that Jake's dad had started when his son was still too young to work the fields. But boys started young in these parts. Most of Jake's male classmates were driving a tractor and working the fields by age 10, startling to city dwellers, typical of life in Conway's farming community. Vera kept the tractor and the implements: a plow and a one-way, a disc and a spring tooth, a chisel and a drill, tools of the trade that Jake could grow into. By the time he was sixteen and my best friend, he worked the land, planted the wheat – with help from an older farmer – and drove a truck during harvest.

In my sixteenth year I experienced my first wheat harvest from the inside, an outsider allowed in, like an alien invited to celebrate the strangeness of an unfamiliar cultural event. Here was the seminal happening of the year in the community and I was asked to attend. The year before I had noticed the increased activity, the energy in early June. Conway and the surrounding roads and fields had awakened, come alive, transformed into a vibrant, bustling place. Big trucks arrived with combines strapped behind their cabs, custom cutters in Conway for a few days before heading north to follow the harvest, their final destination the fields of the Dakotas and beyond to the Canadian plains. More traffic came to town; more cars and trucks parked in front of the diner, downtown Conway still awake, less sleepy when I took a late evening stroll past the crowded pool halls and the brightly lit liquor store, a steady flow of customers going in and out, carrying their alcoholic packages after a thirsty day of work.

I was to be a trucker's helper, riding shot gun, waiting for intermittent bursts of activity. We park in the field and wait. The combine stops, our sign to drive across the harvested yellow stubble and pull up beside the machine, the bed of the truck under the auger, which releases its full bin of wheat in a dusty even flow. My job – other than providing the driver, Jake, with pleasant company – was to climb into the bed of the truck as the stream of seed piled into a pointed, moving, sloping mass, sink into the quicksand, and use an aluminum shovel to scoop and level, filling empty corners, so the next delivery would not overflow the sideboards. The truck fills, sides bulge, and Jake bounces the truck back across the field toward the road. I remain in back, on top of the world, sweating and smiling, looking down from the heights across endless fields, under a cloudless, welcoming, spectacular sky, feeling a part of this yearly liturgy – more than a spectator yet less involved than those whose lives depended on the process that ends here, in these fields, on the Great Plains. I look across the miles of glowing landscape and see other machines, working, threshing, propellers spewing swirling straw and dust behind.

I stand "atop of the load" at harvest time, as Whitman writes.

"The big doors of the country-barn stand open and ready,/The dried grass of the harvest-time loads the slow-drawn wagon,/The clear light plays on the brown gray and green intertinged,/The armfuls are packed to the sagging mow:/I am there...I help...I came stretched atop of the load,/I felt its soft jolts...one leg reclined on the other,/I jump from the cross beams, and seize the clover and timothy,/And roll head over heels, and tangle my hair full of wisps."

The farm year is almost over: cut the grain, work the fields, plant the seeds, watch the vanishing brownness turn to green and finally into the brightness of ripe, fuzzy-headed wheat, the hopeful delivery from combine to truck, the crawling, low-geared trip to town – like Whitman's "slow-drawn" wagon – to wait again, with other trucks lined up for a mile on the road's shoulder, headed toward the grain elevator, the final delivery. I climb down from atop of the load. The wheat is tested and weighed, credited to the Tuckers. We inch toward a tunnel opening, hydraulically lift the bed and spill our sagging load into a grated pit. Return to the scales, Jake pockets the receipt, and we drive, satisfied, back to the field.

After harvest I rode shotgun again in the fields, this time with Jake on a tractor, pulling an implement, around and around in dusty circles, turning the stubble under. Dirt rises to the top, churning upward, and blows away in brown ghosts – the beginning of a hot windy summer as the land is prepared for another planting in early autumn. My teacher lets me take over, like taking a turn behind the wheel in driver's education class. At one point he left me on my own; my teacher abandoned me for a few minutes. I had earned my license. Later in the summer Vera hired me to disc the home quarter. (Jake had other responsibilities.) My new status became official. I was a hired hand, a field worker, a destroyer of a sexist division of labor. I appeared on the list of hired help. I worked the land for other farmers.

My female friends at school were bewildered. Pastor Fred and Jean were skeptical but supportive. My mom thought that field work was unbecoming of a young lady; Pastor Fred thought it would build my Christian character and reinforce the virtues of small town life. I fancied a more romantic image of my introduction to farm life, a more Whitmanesque connection to the soil, two years into my Conway sojourn.

Despite having adult responsibilities Jake never complained or talked as if he was burdened by too much at such a young age. Just the reverse. He evinced a quiet joy about his farm life and the prospects of growing up, stepping in for his father. In the fields, on the Tucker's farm, he was already a man. Of course he loved Vera. But there were two other things he loved above all else: baseball and the farm. I could see the direction of his life. He would graduate from high school, go to college at GPSC, continue to play baseball, and then return to the farm. I was sure of that. Others might drift away from Conway, but not Jake. He was of the farm. Jake would live and die there.

I recall a spring evening of our junior year, on Jake's farm, before harvest. The wheat was in the first stages of ripening, heads reaching toward the sky, waving in a slight breeze, green but soon turning toward its harvest hue. We were walking west on a country road at dusk, holding hands, surrounded by the prosperous hush of the crop lightly swishing, a calm extending flatly to the horizon. We had grown closer: more dates, slow dances, farm tutorials, and at times, somewhat heavier breathing.

Jake was mesmerized by the landscape. Without turning his head toward me, he almost whispered. "Isn't this great?"

"It's very peaceful, isn't it?"

"Yes. This was my dad's favorite time of the year. That's what my mom told me. When the wheat starts to turn."

"You want to be a farmer, don't you?"

"Yeah, I do. But I want to be a pro ballplayer, and I think I'd like to coach. The only way to do that would be to teach, probably math. I could teach and coach and still farm, like Mr. Hadwiger, or Mr. Parker. He used to coach at Conway. How about you?"

"I think I'd like to teach English, like Mrs. Wilson. Maybe go to GPSC."

"Could you see yourself living on a farm?"

"I don't know. Sometimes it feels lonely, isolated. Do you ever feel lonely out here?"

"No, not really. There are neighbors and it's not far from town. I just like the feel of the farm."

"I like it too, Jake. What do you like best?"

"It's been in our family since the Cherokee Strip Land Run. It's Tucker land, a part of our family, and I hope it always will be. And I like the feel of hard work and the dirt. I like to get dirty. Crazy, huh?"

He turned to me and took me into his arms. We lightly kissed and listened to the silence.

I wonder whether my attempt to learn to be a farm girl was, unconsciously, preparatory; perhaps there was beginning to be a glimmer about my future. I might end up profoundly attached to a form of life that now surrounded me. Yet there were also conflicting impulses associated with reading and thinking and desires to be out there, beyond the fields in an unimaginably big old world. For now, I was giving the local a chance to become mine.

The Kirchners became my second family, if I didn't count Vera, my back-up mother, and Jake, no longer just a brother-like friend. The Kirchner household was such a warm and welcoming environment that it was impossible not to feel at home when I visited. I was Ruth's "first new friend" in her first year at Conway High, and despite the one year difference in our ages, she was as much my best female friend as Marcia Little had become, despite my muddling of the logic of "best." Two "bests" are better than one. And Ruth ultimately graduated from "first new friend" and "best high school friend" to FFL, "friend for life."

Ruth often invited me to the Kirchner farm to help with her homework, algebra in ninth grade, then geometry when she became a sophomore. She was beginning to become aware of boys and she was becoming a striking young lady. The Kirchner genes, which had produced a handsome older brother, had produced a tall, slender, dark-haired wonder, shiny green eyes, and a developing figure that would definitely attract the interest of boys.

Ruth knew nothing about sports and had no motivation to learn, so that area was off limits when we chatted. But she knew I had become the star of the girls basketball team and she insisted that the family attend my games to cheer for me and the Conway Lady Tornadoes. John and Virginia were nice about attending – never a grumble or complaint. They were deeply congenial people, characterized by a genuine Christian agreeableness that sought to please their daughter and prohibited them from saying anything bad about a type of activity – playing organized, competitive sports – that was not allowed for their children. Ruth looked up to me and I adored her. And I appreciated the Kirchners' muted, uninvolved clapping when I scored.

It was nice to have a fan club, including Sarah, now ten years old, who was going through a patch of bad health that winter: a persistent cough, a paler complexion, her childhood chubbiness diminished because she seemed to be losing weight. She looked unhealthy. During our games, most of the kids her age couldn't sit still. Sarah sat with her parents, passive, listless, so unlike her usual energetic demeanor. When I sat with the Kirchners to watch Jake and the Tornado boys play after the girls game, I couldn't get her involved.

Josh was also there at our basketball games, as well as fall and spring baseball games, at least when his busy farm labor schedule permitted. He was a fan, as well as the third member of an exclusive sports club committed to playing and practicing and talking about these joyful games, despite not being allowed to participate in the real thing. To be a member, along with Lizzie and Jake, you had to love sports, which was an odd requirement for Josh since his father was against competition, and the son had faith in his father's faith. No organized competition for Josh, but he could join us for play – enthusiastically, with no self-doubts.

Josh had grown another inch, dark-haired, like Ruth, the same slender Kirchner body, with broad, muscular shoulders and arms – from farm work – a slender waist, long legs, pleasant features: perfect gleaming teeth, rounded cheekbones, a smile that turned up broadly and reached toward dimpled lines, bright green eyes like Ruth's, a thick nose, prominent ears. I had seen a smile like that on a baseball card of the young Mickey Mantle, a face that said "yes" to life. Mickey was a compacted source of wound-tight kinetic energy, less than six feet tall. Josh was now a lithe and agile six feet three, almost graceful, developing in that direction, a fine athletic specimen of the species *Homo sapiens*. John and Virginia made fine babies!

We played at the Tucker farm: catch, hoops, football punting and kicking games, pass patterns. We played on the concrete basketball courts behind the school: H-O-R-S-E, Knock-out, Odd Man (now Person) Out. Josh's basketball skills were improving; he entertained us with his dunks.

Each weekend during baseball season, fall and spring, we met at the Conway High baseball field for our own version of practice. Jake had borrowed a left-handed glove from a graduated high school friend, now in college, so Josh no longer was forced to play awkwardly with wrong-handed leather. We began by playing catch in the outfield. First, short toss. Back up. Then stretch out the arm with long toss. We played a game in which we backed up a step with each throw. If your toss didn't arrive on the fly or the receiver had to take a step to catch the ball, you were out. It wasn't fair – Josh always won. He could throw a baseball on a line from the foul line to the opposite fence.

I hit grounders to Jake at shortstop, who threw across the diamond to Josh, playing first base. Jake hit flies to the outfielders, Josh and Lizzie, who came up firing to home plate. We taught him: in the outfield throw overhand, get on top, to make the ball carry straight, no fade. (Coach Ross had taught that.) Josh taught us: this is how you chase a fly with long, fluid strides and catch a ball that shouldn't be caught.

We took batting practice: a pitcher, a shagger, and a hitter. Ten cuts. Three rounds. Keep things moving.

We ended with something just for Josh. We had started more specialized pitching practice in the Tucker backyard, plenty of space for throwing, with a slightly raised part of the yard that was an apt replica of a pitching mound. We dug a piece of wood into the ground to be a pitching rubber. Jake was the catcher, I stood at an improvised home plate, with a bat, to offer a more realistic representation of a strike zone, and Josh was our All-Star left-hander. Toe the rubber, turn the hips, leg kick to the waist, a stride toward home plate, an easy, effortless delivery, the ball on top of me quickly, the crack of the catcher's mitt when Jake caught it just right.

We worked on pitch counts, as if Josh was pitching in a real game. Jake was already a good coach. We worked on location. We worked on different grips and different pitches. His curve ball wasn't much; his change-up wouldn't fool anyone because he slowed his arm speed too much. He needed better pitching coaches. But his fast ball needed no help. It was alive, with natural movement. Nature, or God, had given him a gift – was it destined to be an unopened package? Jake and I had a secret: a pitcher who might take the Tornadoes to the state tournament. He was, for now, nothing but a blank cartridge – and a charter member of our secret athletic club.

I see her walk into the classroom that first day of school: Junior English, with Jake, Marcia, and friends. She steps confidently to the front of the room, places her book and class register on the desk, and introduces herself in a pleasant tone, careful to look in the direction of each student, front to back: "I'm Mrs. Wilson, and this is a course on American Literature."

There is no apparent nervousness. Unlike her predecessor, Miss Turner, she seems at ease in front of a group of teenage egoists, for whom their present location, where they happen to be at the moment, is the center of a chummy universe, and whose lives had not yet acquired ragged edges. We hadn't learned how to be perpetually anxious or depressed. My classmates were, for the most part, happy, optimistic, confident, and uncomplicated. I probably took Jake as my model. Mrs. Wilson was there to introduce some complexity into an otherwise unreflective, practical mode of human existence: a 1966 instantiation of insular life in Conway, Oklahoma, USA.

Mrs. Wilson was a normal size youthful-looking woman, mid 30s, not large, not small, nothing for the boys to make fun of – nothing for the rude, immature humor of my male classmates to latch on to, as they did when Mrs. Gordon glided through the hallways, her 300-something pounds of hips and rear end swaying impressively and forcefully, side to side, like a sumo wrestler in a rustling skirt doing a hula dance. Mrs. Gordon was the object of merciless crudeness. Mrs. Wilson would invoke in her students other emotions: respect bordering on fear, and puppy love.

Her brown hair was cut stylishly short; her earrings were oversized hoops. There was nothing remarkable about her features except her eyes: blue, large, and round, alert and intelligent, framed by studious-looking rimless glasses that made her look older. Pretty – the north side of plain, south of beautiful. Her body was well-proportioned without calling attention to itself. A modest skirt cut just so; a white blouse (she often wore a white blouse) buttoned high on her neck, a sign of some modesty. She spoke deliberately, articulately, with a hint of southern sophistication and precise enunciation that sent me scurrying, after class, to a dictionary in the library to look up unfamiliar high-brow words. Her speech was more impressive than her external appearance.

There was an aura of seriousness and quiet intensity as she looked at us and demanded our attention. Her bearing reminded me of a toned-down preacher who attempted to convey enthusiasm for the Word, yet she delivered her passion for Literature with a disciplined self-control. Unlike a preacher, her serious-ness was seasoned with a tone of playfulness and detachment, an irony unknown to God's professionals, like Pastor Fred. She seemed to be playing a kind of game with us, whose rules we were to learn from her; she hoped we would learn to love the game as she did. At times a pleasant expression was on the verge of overcoming her studied reserve, not quite a big smile – if we were able to please her with our shallow answers to her deep questions.

As the fall term progressed I became more and more fas-cinated by Mrs. Wilson. I wanted to know more about her; I wanted to know how she ended up teaching at Conway High School. How did she become interested in literature? I began dropping by her classroom when she had a planning period, or after school. She never turned me away.

When we talked she looked directly into my eyes, as if there was nothing more interesting than what I happened to be saying or the questions I asked.

"I was a reader, Lizzie. One of my teachers said there were two kinds of people in the world. There are readers, people who always refer to some specific book when you ask, 'what are you reading?' They are always reading something. And there are those for whom the written word is less a friend than a stranger."

"What did you read when you were my age?"

"In high school, mostly fiction. Later, in college and after I graduated, I read everything: literature, history, biography, cur-rent affairs, philosophy, religion, popular fiction, science."

"When did you decide you wanted to be an English teacher?"

"After I went to college. I grew up in Tulsa. My dad was a businessman and my mom a homemaker, but they were both readers and they encouraged me. I had a library card when I was very young."

"Where did you go to college?"

"I went to the University of Kansas for two years until the money ran out when my dad's business failed. The University of Kansas is a beautiful campus, high on a hill overlooking Lawrence. It's so gorgeous in the spring, when the hyacinth blooms and the tulips and the daffodils flower, and the crabapple trees explode with color – and there were magnificent green open spaces on the hillsides, and a charming downtown with a great second-hand bookstore. It would be a good place for you to go to college, Lizzie."

"But you had to leave?"

"Yes. After two years in Lawrence I went back to Tulsa to work and read for a year. At the University of Kansas I had a fine course on Victorian literature with a wonderful teacher. I spent months back in Tulsa reading Dickens, Charlotte and Emily Bronte, George Eliot, Thomas Hardy, Thackeray – thousands of pages of grand storytelling and passion."

"Then what?"

"I moved to Alma and lived with my grandparents to save money. By that time I decided I wanted to be an English teacher. I majored in Language Arts Education at Great Plains State College. There was a strong English Department there, but I think I was most influenced by a teacher in the Department of Humanities and Religion. He still teaches at GPSC. I took four courses from him, including two philosophy courses. They opened my eyes to a different kind of thinking."

"Philosophy. I don't think I understand what philosophy is."

"It's difficult to explain. Perhaps I'll introduce you some day to Professor Taylor. I'm sure he would like to talk to you about philosophy."

"So, after you graduated from GPSC, where did you teach?"

"I met my football-playing husband at GPSC and after graduation and marriage we moved from school to school as my husband – he teaches social studies and coaches – advanced in the world of high school football. He was hired to be Head Football Coach at Alma High School, there was an English position open at Conway High, so here I am. And I've picked up some graduate courses in English along the way."

"Do you want to stay at Conway High School?"

"We'll see. I love teaching – especially interested and motivated students."

Miss Turner's mismatched career choice turned into Mrs. Wilson's opportunity, another mismatch.

Mrs. Wilson may not have been a Big Leaguer, but she was at least a Double A or Triple A player assigned to a Rookie League. At Conway she was assigned to the wrong level. Her job was to raise the level of play for all of us, despite our limitations. Her goal was to get out of the bush leagues, finish her advanced degree, perhaps be hired at GPSC as an adjunct, excel in her teaching, overpower the opposition, and achieve a full-time college teaching position as a Lecturer. On the way, class members in Junior American Literature, Conway High School, would be the practice squad. I was lucky; most of my classmates were not so fortunate. Her pedagogical techniques were too advanced for many of her students, until, at one point in the second semester, she gave up on literature (for a few weeks) and instituted Writing Bootcamp, sans Lizzie, who was sent away on her own to read, to meet Holden Caulfield and to enter Vonnegut's strange funhouse.

She embodied a type of person, a "character" I would encounter and appreciate, although, at the time, the concept was unavailable to me. She was an Intellectual, the first I had ever encountered. Mr. Ross was aware, historically literate and engaged in the world, a knowledgeable and informed American citizen and member of the Cherokee Nation, but I sensed that ideas and books were at the center of Mrs. Wilson's life in a more essential way. She astonished us – no, she astonished me – with the breadth of her learning and her desire to know more and more, to seek to become acquainted with all parts of the library. Her own personal library dominated the walls of her home in Alma, floor to ceiling built-in bookshelves, stacked and crammed. Once, she led me through the labyrinth, an experienced tour guide, a path of discovery through her books.

"Lizzie, look around. So many books! How does the library make you feel? Isn't it glorious? When I walk into this room it almost takes my breath away."

"Have you read all of these books?"

"No, I haven't read all of them, but I've read many of them. And those I haven't read are there for the future, for inspiration or study or reference. After I read a book I want to possess it. It shows me where I've been, what I've thought about, what I've felt, what I have accomplished. Once I read a book I feel as if I have a personal relationship with the author. Do you ever feel that way?"

"Yes, when I read Whitman and Cather. Sometimes I think they're talking directly to me."

"When I'm here I'm sure that I will never be bored or feel alone. Emily Dickinson expressed something like that, but about the birds and her garden. For me, the library puts me in the presence of people I want to believe are like me, and I'm here to be with them and share their thoughts. The library makes me feel curious and grateful – and very humble. Can you sense what I mean?"

"Yes, Mrs. Wilson. When I read great writers in your class I'm often amazed, when there's some beautiful passage or collection of words that paints a scene so well – or describes characters so perfectly that I feel I can reach out and talk to them although they aren't real."

"The library also shows me there is another world than the one we can see and smell and touch. It's a world of ideas, and I often think that it's more important and more real than the physical one – because it's the world that guides our life and fires our most cherished values and gives us hope – and meaning."

We were silent for a few moments. I wasn't sure I followed her. I didn't know what to say.

"Lizzie, if there's meaning in life, for me it resides in the library. Its meanings radiate outward and light up the world!"

I was attracted to her form of life. She was approachable, yet she didn't want to be our friend – or, in my case, after some time, she really did want to be my friend but she wouldn't allow herself to indulge a desire incompatible with her role. She maintained a proper distance between us, teacher and student. She refused the possibility of advancing to another kind of friendship; the boundaries were established by age, experience, learning, and role. She wanted to be our teacher, to introduce us to the pleasures of American Literature. But she became, for me, a Teacher, the one who might change a life, re-direct a path, initiate a new way, enliven nascent inclinations and interests.

I took to her and she took to me. Early on I told her I had read Whitman and wondered if she could help me understand more about his poetry. "Will we be reading Whitman?"

She was incredulous. "You have read Whitman? Of course we'll read Whitman."

I told her the story of Charles DuPont and my friend Harry Berens.

"That's marvelous," she said.

Was she a role model for me? I detest the notion of a "role model," not because the notion is inapt in a young life, but because it is facile. Coach Ross was a role model, despite being male and Native American. We don't have to see ourselves in the most popular cultural and political modes of identification to be inspired and attracted to others' qualities. We resemble others in innumerable ways and it is up to us to choose – or to be chosen by – the categories of identity that connect with us most deeply. Mrs. Wilson wasn't my role model because she was a bright, stylish, educated female teacher; she was a role model because she lived in a world of ideas.

My journal records details of our junior year with Mrs. Wilson: readings, assignments, new vocabulary, questions. Yet these specific elements coalesce into impressions, distinctive emotional colors that are more vivid than particulars: excitement, frustration, curiosity, wonder – the experience of interrogating life in a new way, being involved in something bigger, much different from my involvement with Pastor Fred's worldview or the fate of the St. Louis Cardinals. Her course dominated my life. She demanded to be a part of each weeknight, with reading and writing assignments. She gave us a new vocabulary to wield as we attempted to decipher the meanings of poems and short stories – and a novel – written by geniuses who shared our history and traditions. I cherish those experiences with Mrs. Wilson: unique, unrepeatable, and seismic. One of my two favorite authors in that year of awakening, Willa Cather, identifies the significance of the past: "Some memories are realities, and are better than anything that can ever happen to one again."

Some particular memories remain, probably because benign conflicts and disagreements serve to highlight moments of experience in which a self is tested. Mrs. Wilson loved the poetry of Emily Dickinson more than my favorite poet. They were editorially linked in a section of our text called "The Modern Temper," successors to "Planters and Puritans," "Founders of the Nation," the "Early National Period," a "Renaissance" dominated by Emerson and Thoreau, and the "End of an Era" that predated Modernism. She admired Whitman as "our first modern poet," and she praised his unique voice, but she preferred Dickinson's poems, usually much shorter than Whitman's. Her poems were opaque, puzzling, cramped, formally tight, written with a common meter and cerebral symbols, and much more obscure. I tried to love what Mrs. Wilson loved but I could not penetrate the rigor and symbolic obscurity of Dickinson's work. I much preferred Whitman's long, expressive breathless lines, his adventurous meter, his passion for the ordinary, his lyrical images of everydayness, and his exclamation points – more powerful than her annoying dashes. I preferred his vigor to her rigor. His poetry seemed to me, in my youthful ardor, to express freedom and individuality. His writing about God and nature and the self and death seemed to affirm life; her poems about anguish, love, and death appeared to describe a life closed-off from the world, secluded in a drawing room, private, resisting Whitman's attempt to spread out, to stretch and sweat. They shared topics but not sensibilities. Whitman was crude and untutored in a way that excited me; Dickinson's poetry made me nervous. I'm sure that Mrs. Wilson thought I was intellectually ill-prepared to do justice to Dickinson's cognitive originality and depth, yet my Whitmanesque youthful tastes survived into adulthood. Sometimes artless readings are better.

In the spring we read *My Antonia*, by Willa Cather. I can never re-read her book without thinking of Mrs. Wilson, my new boyfriend Jake, and what it feels like to grow up on the Great Plains, with scorching summer heat, warm, clear, autumn days that turn crisp in the evening, eye-watering Arctic fronts that come barreling down the plains, and lush spring days fit for baseball and walking through a pasture and the threat of afternoon thunderstorms.

My favorite part of *My Antonia* was Book I, "The Shimerdas," where Cather first depicts Antonia, the Bohemian girl who came to symbolize the harsh realities of making a life out of nothing but the possibility of turning a plains wilderness into something livable and prosperous. It was Cather the prose-poet that I loved best, when she described the land and the seasons that felt familiar and welcoming, yet frightful and lonely.

"As I looked about me I felt the grass was the country, as water is the sea. The red of the grass made all the great prairie the color of wine-stains, or of certain seaweeds when they are first washed up. And there was so much motion in it; the whole country seemed, somehow, to be running."

Our waving wheat was like Cather's prairie grass, whose motion was, indeed, like the perpetual motion of the sea. Her trees were like ours: "Some of the cottonwoods had already turned, and the yellow leaves and shining white bark made them look like the gold and silver trees in fairy tales." Our fall afternoons: "As far as we could see, the miles of copper-red-grass were drenched in sunlight that was stronger and fiercer than at any other time of day." The first snowfall. The first country Christmas. A beautiful spring morning. In July, "that breathless brilliant heat which makes the plains of Kansas and Nebraska the best corn country in the world." A "beautiful electric storm," in which "the thunder was loud and metallic, like the rattle of sheet iron, and the lightning broke in great zigzags across the heavens, making everything stand out and come close to us for a moment." Her prose was clear and graceful, luminous and soothing, despite the harshness and the extremes, the uneducated forces of nature. And Antonia was as strong and powerful as the place she inhabited.

Jake hated the book; we argued for the first time about something other than baseball-related matters. Was Mantle better than Mays, Musial better than Williams?

"It's a dumb book."

"No, it's not a dumb book. It's a beautiful book."

"Nothing happens."

"What happens is not as important as the way that Cather evokes a place and a way of life and the character of people who have to confront how hard pioneer life is, like Antonia."

"It's boring. Antonia is nice to Jim, loves her dad, learns to speak English. Her dad hates the place and commits suicide. Her mother is envious and nasty; her brother is a jerk. The 'hired girls' move to town and turn wild. Antonia gets in trouble, has a baby, and finally finds a husband and has a lot of kids. Boring!"

I insisted that Cather's book is beautiful, but I had a difficult time explaining what I meant – to him, and to me – and how much I was touched by the female characters, especially Antonia. I identified with her, despite her bad choices and lack of education. Jake saw weakness in her; I saw strength.

Cather left me with vivid images, none more so than her description of Antonia's children, when Jim Burden visited her farm twenty years after he had last seen her. The children enthusiastically show Jim their new fruit cave.

"We turned to leave the cave; Antonia and I went up the stairs first, and the children waited. We were standing outside talking, when they all came running up the steps together, big and little, tow heads and gold heads and brown, and flashing little naked legs; a veritable explo-

sion of life out of the dark cave into the sunlight. It made me dizzy for a moment."

I visited that cave years later, north of Red Cloud, Nebraska, and saw what the narrator saw, in my Cather-affected imagination. I could also imagine why Jim found the scene rich with meaning.

"That moment, when they all came tumbling out of that cave into the light, was a sight any man might have come far to see. Antonia had always been one to leave images in the mind that did not fade – that grew stronger with time. In my memory there was a succession of such pictures, fixed like the old woodcuts of one's first primer... She lent herself to immemorial human attitudes which we recognize by instinct as universal and true. I had not been mistaken. She was a battered woman now, not a lovely girl; but she still had that something which fires the imagination, could still stop one's breath for a moment by a look or gesture that somehow revealed the meaning in common things."

Perhaps the beauty of her writing was to convey memories and images, "fixed like old woodcuts of one's first primer," as vividly as moments of my life in Conway, here and now, the ability to reveal "the meaning in common things." I find in my journal, at the time, my new theory of beauty: "a pleasing vividness, a lucid clarity that demands one's attention, that sends you out of yourself to apprehend something – a scene, an object – or a perfect representation of it."

One day in late spring Mrs. Wilson ended class by giving us a reading assignment, which was typical, and making an announcement. "For tomorrow I want you to read a poem we skipped." She turned and wrote the title of the poem on the chalkboard: "The Love Song of J. Alfred Prufrock."

"It's a very famous poem, and a very difficult poem. You should read it more than once. Read it slowly. I have invited a distinguished visitor, a college professor, for tomorrow's class, to help us understand this poem, and to talk briefly about what it's like to go to college."

That night I read the poem. It was incomprehensible. I read it again. Who is Prufrock? He seems to be middle-aged; he says he has a "bald spot in the middle of my hair." He wears a "coat" and a "necktie." He's bothered by other people: "the eyes that fix you in a formulated phrase." He describes his location in creepy, yellow metaphors. He's not a happy man; he may be depressed. "I have seen the moment of my greatness flicker." He doesn't seem to know what to do. "And indeed there will be time/To wonder, 'Do I dare?' and, 'Do I dare?'"

When we walked into class next day our visitor was standing next to Mrs. Wilson. "I would like to introduce Professor Enos Taylor, from Great Plains State College. He was one of my teachers." She pauses and turns to him. "Actually, he was my favorite teacher. Today he would like to talk to us about this puzzling poem by T. S. Eliot. And I've asked him to save the last few minutes to talk about GPSC and what college experience is like."

I imagined a college professor would be intimidating and we wouldn't be able to understand anything he said. I wasn't sure what Mrs. Wilson was up to. Intimidating? Obscure? Head in an indecipherable cloud of abstractions? None of the above. In fact, just the opposite. He was a small man, short but wiry, thinning hair, round wire-rimmed glasses, corduroy coat, open collar, blue jeans, desert boots, studious looking, like his student, Mrs. Wilson. He was genial and welcoming, with a warm smile and a fluid conversational style that put us at ease. He seemed like one of us – which, it turned out, he was. He grew up on a farm north of Alma, between the city limits and the Kansas border. I would learn more about his story in September, when I sat in on one of his classes and talked to him on campus.

I expected him to lecture. Instead, he spent much of his time asking questions and responding to what we said – to what I said, since my classmates were not very talkative. Later in class, when he did fall into something akin to a lecture, his explanations were more like telling us a story than reciting key points about what it might have been like to confront societal changes in the early part of the twentieth century.

He began by asking us what poets and writers we especially liked in our course on American Literature. A few moments of silence. I raised my hand.

"I especially like Whitman, Robert Frost, two short stories, one by Willa Cather, the other by Eudora Welty, and I love *My Antonia*, by Cather."

"Your name?"

"Lizzie Ware."

"Well, Lizzie, can you tell me what you like about those authors? How about Whitman?"

We started a conversation. He asked more questions.

"Let's hear from someone else." Silence. He smiled and pointed at one of my classmates.

"How about you? What's your name?"

"Chris."

"So, Chris, what about you? What have you liked?"

"Nothin'. I don't really like to read." A few chuckles.

"What do you like to do?"

"I like to hunt and fish and watch TV." We laughed.

"You know what, Chris? I like to hunt and fish, too. I can see your point."

Professor Taylor broke the ice, but it was a struggle for him to get others engaged. He tried. How old is Prufrock? Describe his physical appearance. What is he like? Can you describe his personality? We read passages. What does Prufrock mean here? He helped. He nudged. He praised. "That's interesting." What is Prufrock's relation to others? What is his mood? What is the feeling you get from the poem? What do you make of these metaphors? He led us, or I should say, he led me, to understand more about Eliot's great poem.

As much as he wanted to engage everyone, the class devolved into a dialogue between Professor Taylor and me. When he tried to sum up by giving us a sense of modernism, a growing sensibility characterized by alienation from society and other people, I asked about the differences between Prufrock's tortured inner life, his anxieties and despair, and Whitman, who, as Mrs. Wilson had claimed, was the first "modern poet." "Excellent question, Lizzie." And he proceeded to answer my question with a question for me, so it seemed that I was answering my own question.

I found the class exhilarating; Jake said he was bored. I could see the influence of Professor Taylor on Mrs. Wilson. I could see in him what she might have seen when she encountered a master teacher and devotee of the unseen world of ideas. I could see how I might be excited about reading and thinking, as well as playing games.

After class I approached Professor Taylor like a fan approaching a famous baseball player, gushing, saying how great he was and how much the fan loved watching him play.

"Are you named after Enos Slaughter?"

"Who?" He had never heard of Enos Slaughter.

I asked him what classes he taught at GPSC.

"I teach courses in the humanities, and I teach two courses in philosophy: an introductory course and a course in ethics. Perhaps you would like to sit in on one of my courses?"

"I would."

"I teach 'Introduction to Philosophy' in the fall term. I schedule it in late afternoon, 5:00 until 6:15, two days a week, so older students in town and in the area can fit it into a busy work schedule – my contribution to adult education in the community. I could send you the syllabus. Mrs. Wilson took the course. I suspect she still has the texts."

"I do." Mrs. Wilson smiled.

"That would be great."

"Fine. Then perhaps I'll see you in September!"

What was Mrs. Wilson's intent that day? No doubt she wanted to show off her mentor, and she wanted to show us what it was like to be in a college classroom. But she was already a teacher who resembled that model and most students in class were incapable of appreciating what we had experienced in the wise and masterful handling of a poem whose very difficulty was part of its fame and allure. No, I think her intent was stealthier. I think she wanted me to meet Professor Enos Taylor, and I think she wanted him to meet me. I think she saw in me some hidden talent that might be discovered in a tiny town, like Tom Greenwade saw in Mickey Mantle. As Coach Ross would teach me, baseball scouts see the future. Talent must be nurtured and developed. Mickey signed young, but he had the ability, just graduated from high school, to play in the minor leagues. In September I might find myself playing at a higher level.

I replay this scene in my mind. It's very much like the day I found out that Harry had died. I walk into the house after school. This time it's only my mom who is the bearer of bad news. My dad is pastoring somewhere. I can tell something is wrong.

"I have some very sad news, Lizzie. Sarah Kirchner died this morning."

Little Sarah, barely ten years old. Bubbly, lively, energetic – at least until the last few weeks. I had seen neither Josh nor Ruth in school that day; at the time, their absence didn't strike me as odd. I hadn't been out to the Kirchner farm in two or three weeks. I knew Sarah hadn't been doing well. I asked Ruth and Josh fairly regularly, "How's Sarah?" Not so great. She had lost weight, felt weak and lethargic, had a constant cough, drank a lot of water. She wasn't getting better. I asked about a doctor.

"Has she seen Dr. Little? What does he say about her?"

Ruth told me that her parents hadn't taken Sarah to a doctor. "We don't believe in doctors. We don't believe that medicine can heal us. We believe we can heal ourselves through our prayers and the prayers of other people in our family and church. Illness isn't real."

I reconstructed the final days. John and Virginia Kirchner had prayed their special prayers. They believed they were giving Sarah spiritual treatment: faith healing. They invited a distinguished, paid Christian Scientist practitioner to the farm to help treat Sarah's illness, to offer more prayers. Sarah's health worsened. The last day she went into a coma. Still no doctor. More prayers. Sarah died.

Marcia told me about her father's reactions. When Dr. Little heard about Sarah's symptoms, his diagnosis was immediate: probably childhood diabetes, treatable – he called it a "senseless death."

Two weeks later, the pallor of Sarah's death still hovering in our lives, another untimely death, this time after extended medical treatment. Eight-year-old Andrew Waters, a member of our congregation, died of a cancer of the blood. Like the Kirchners, we had prayed for Andrew's health; unlike the Kirchners, Andrew's family had wisely decided to enlist modern medicine to help with whatever God had in mind. The mystery of childhood death and illness in God's Plan remained unsolved, residue left over from failed prayers and scientific intervention and unshakable faith that "everything is for the best in the best of all possible worlds."

When Harry died, my faith in God's infinite love convinced me that the myth of the faithless being sent to Hell was wrong. If God loves us, then he understands his creatures. He wouldn't send them to an eternity of suffering. That's not love; it sounds more like a tyrant wielding his power in unconscionable ways as preachers wave a stick at us and poke us to provoke our fears.

Throughout my childhood I had heard Pastor Fred describe God as infinitely loving and infinitely powerful. His love for us through Jesus Christ's power to forgive our sins is unsurpassable, as is His power to do absolutely anything. We prayed for Him to intervene in the life of a child – or the lives of parents whose love for their child was a perfect image of God's love for us. God loved Sarah, and He loved John and Virginia. He could have counteracted what was going on in her body, or he could have placed a strange idea in their minds. *"Take your daughter to a physician, just this one time. We must try to do more to save your little girl."* If He's there, wouldn't this have been possible? Couldn't He have altered Andrew's blood, destroyed the cancer, and allowed him to live? Couldn't He have put a more effective protocol in the minds of cancer researchers, years ahead of schedule?

I began to think of God as a bystander. An innocent bystander? How could He be innocent if his love was infinite and his power unsurpassable? I could not see how childhood suffering and death could be part of God's Plan. We prayed…and there was silence. I had to admit, despite years of Pastor Fred's preaching and instructions, for me – for Lizzie Ware – God was hidden. When Harry died I began to formulate the heretical notion that God's love rendered our belief in God superfluous. It doesn't matter whether we're Christians or Muslims or Buddhists or atheists; it doesn't even matter whether we believe in Him, as long as we're good. As Harry said, "You don't need religion to be good."

Now, Sarah's death and Andrew's death left me with even more uncomfortable possibilities. Surely God knew about their illnesses. Yet they suffered and died too young. Therefore, either God didn't love them, even as much as I loved them or their parents loved them; or He couldn't do anything about their illnesses. Either God isn't infinitely loving or God isn't infinitely powerful. Or, worst of all, He isn't there.

| **five** |

Scouting, Philosophy, and Chance

For weeks after Sarah's death I wasn't quite right. In retrospect, her death was a marker for me. I found myself taking long walks at night, around town, often out on a country road, headed toward the Tucker's farm, thinking, wondering. On Sundays I was more uncomfortable hearing my father preach with utter certainty that he knew God's intentions and purposes. If Pastor Fred couldn't explain why an innocent child had to suffer and die, if he could only say that we must have faith that there is a reason for everything that happens in God's kingdom, then his certainties were empty; my doubts couldn't be stilled. My father's confidence disturbed me; he was incapable of understanding me and what I was thinking.

I was vaguely aware that something important was happening to me but I wasn't sure about its meaning. It was like going on a vacation, feeling you are having an adventure. There's a beginning and you're taken up by the flow of time. There's a sense that you are in the middle of a story and someday you will be able to recount it, yet in the moment its direction and end are unknown. The attempt to bring the adventure into a satisfying unity is fallible, prone to misinterpretation and reconsideration. It's hopeless to attempt to narrate the meaning of the story prematurely but the desire to understand what is happening is unavoidable.

Sarah's death changed my relation to Conway; her passing represented something I didn't want to admit. Conway was safe and comfortable. Conway was narrow and predictable. Conway was in my bones; its rhythm and scenes had eaten into my soul. On my walks I told myself how wonderful it is to love a place, to have a home. I sensed that it would never leave me; the question was whether I would leave Conway. My high school years were a prelude to a life I was trying to imagine as I sifted through alternative possibilities. Whether I left or stayed, life in Conway would leave me with impressions and images that were like deposits of precious metals that could be mined at will and would, at inopportune times, demand to be mined.

I was fascinated by the beginning of Book III in *My Antonia*, in which the narrator, Jim Burden, leaves the country, escapes from the small prairie town of Black Hawk, Antonia and the hired girls, and attends the university in Lincoln, Nebraska. He rents two small rooms on the edge of town, overlooking the open country, and lives the life of a student scholar in a space filled with books, decorated with a "map of ancient Rome," and a "photograph of the Tragic Theatre at Pompei." He comes under the influence of a mentor, a young classics professor who assists him in his time of "mental awakening," one of the happiest times in his life, he says. "Gaston Cleric introduced me to the world of ideas; when one first encounters that world everything else fades for a time, and all that went before is as if it had not been. Yet I found curious survivals; some of the figures of my old life seemed to be waiting for me in the new."

I imagined I would be like Jim Burden. Leave the confines of Conway; throw myself into an adventure of ideas in a college town. Jim stayed up late talking with Gaston Cleric, "about Latin and English poetry, or telling me about his long stay in Italy." He thought his mentor "narrowly missed being a great poet." Mrs. Wilson and Professor Enos Taylor had given me a first taste. What would it be like to throw myself into an intellectual life?

Jim Burden found out he couldn't be a scholar. He followed his mentor to Harvard, then became a lawyer. Yet his time in Lincoln was exhilarating and necessary. It clarified his relation to the impersonality of abstract ideas and the importance of his "own infinitesimal past." How would Conway enter my future? Would it be as my own infinitesimal past, filling my memory, "which I wanted to crowd with other things," or would it become the comfortable assurance of everydayness?

My two best friends – one of whom was now my boyfriend and someone I was beginning to love – represented the tug of opposites in my life. Jake was Conway, the farm, baseball, and the Great Plains. He knew what he wanted and where the story would end. He wanted to be a ballplayer and he was already a farmer. He said he'd kill for the chance to play professional baseball. Even if that happened, after baseball he would return to the farm. He would never really leave. Unlike Jim Burden, Jake's infinitesimal past would be continuous with his present and future, a satisfying unity in which he knows every tree, the slope and texture of each field, the history of each person he passes in Conway as he travels to and from the small town he inhabits and the land he loves.

My other best friend was Marcia Little, rich girl, the Doctor's daughter, somewhat snooty and condescending, a city kid sent to live in the land of bib overalls, open vistas, dust, and eternal wind – a stranger who wanted out. She overcame her class-bound suspicions of the Preacher's Kid. She liked my openness to new things, my "experimental attitude." She was in awe of my athletic ability and respected my intelligence: "Lizzie, you're so smart." Marcia found out that I loved music and played the guitar and piano and decided to take charge of my tastes. She championed Bob Dylan, the British Invasion, and the Beatles. When a new Beatles record came out she was first in line at Newman's, the music store in Alma. I was the only person invited to the concert in her bedroom. I had a ticket to hear John, George, Paul, and Ringo on her compact stereo record player, with separated speakers. Pastor Fred and Jean had no idea what was going on when I escaped to Marcia's alienated space, far from Conway.

Marcia was a caricature of a high school girl trying to be cool and different. When we heard that John Lennon said the Beatles were more popular than Jesus, she laughed and said, "It's true!" I knew I was supposed to be scandalized – and she was trying to scandalize me – but her counter-Conway zeal was infectious. John Lennon's comment – and Marcia's attitude – appeared in a sermon at the Methodist church condemning the ungodly decadence of American society: Conway as the locus of societal decline.

For a Conway girl, Marcia was worldly and experienced – at least she pretended to be. She fancied herself a cosmopolitan, a citizen from out there. The Littles had money to travel: weekends in Tulsa and Oklahoma City for music and plays; summer vacations to exciting places: Los Angeles, San Diego, Chicago, and even a trip to France. The summer before our senior year the Littles were spending a week in New York City, for Broadway shows, cultured trips to museums, and high-class cuisine. There was a chance I might be asked to go with the Littles to New York.

In the lives of my two best friends, Conway acted as contrary forces: for Jake, a centripetal attraction acting in the direction of the center; for Marcia, a powerful centrifugal force directed outward, toward an open future rather than a deadened past. I was caught between two forces.

The content of conversations with my best friends reflected two different realities. For one: baseball, farming, and the minutia of an agricultural community on the plains. "We sure need rain." "The wheat is lookin' pretty good." "Did you hear that Olen Mullins is in the hospital?" "How about that Lizzie Ware? She scored over thirty points the other night."

In the other world there were civil rights marches, bombs falling in Vietnam, Peter, Paul, and Mary singing protest songs, Bob Dylan's inspiring but confounding lyrics and the excitement in June 1967, of "Sgt. Pepper's Lonely Hearts Club Band" being released. By the end of the summer it had sold over 2 million copies, one of which was being played in a house in Conway, two seventeen year old girls convinced they were listening to the greatest rock album in history.

Beyond high school graduation, most students in Conway chose one of two options: attend the local college in Alma or go to work. One recent grad went to Okmulgee Tech to study diesel mechanics; another ventured to Oklahoma State University to study poultry science.

Marcia was destined to go to the University of Oklahoma, to flee, to study who knows what. We could go together, she said. I could major in English, I thought. Get a room. Drink coffee late at night. Have deep intellectual conversations. I would be like Jim Burden. But what about Jake?

I can't recall the precise moment my scouting lessons began. They didn't have exact starting times or locations, unlike my guitar sessions with Harry or my piano lessons with Vera Tucker. Coach Ross had told me baseball stories about Tom Greenwade and Mickey Mantle, his scuffles in the low minor leagues, and how he became a bird-dog scout, working with Greenwade and the Yankees. He had been offered a full-time job scouting for the Cardinals – at the behest of his friend's recommendation – but he declined. Low pay. Too much travel away from home. He loved coaching and teaching. But he was a scout. He was a baseball guy. He knew the lingo and he loved schmoozing with other scouts. I wanted him to teach me. I didn't see why a woman couldn't be a scout. Instead of a Whitman scholar, maybe I could become a baseball scout.

My lessons started sporadically, with off-hand comments on the ballfield or in the bleachers. There were some other teaching venues, including mini-lectures, tutorials in Coach Ross's tiny cubicle, behind the gym, down the stairs, tucked between the girls and boys locker rooms, a distinctive feel for my instruction: damp, sticky, exposed pipes, locker room smells invading our privacy, sensory remnants of sweating bodies, communal showers, and ripening workout clothes hanging in exposed wooden lockers. My first morsels of scouting wisdom had a distinctive scent.

After a scouting tutorial I wrote notes. I can hear his gentle voice. I carried his lessons to our first scouting road trip in the spring of my junior year. Apart from a ball field, his instruction was like an introductory class in art history. The teacher tells students what to look for before the lights are dimmed, the screen descends, and the images appear at the front of the classroom. The real education takes place at the ballpark, when a pre-existing mental set is applied to individuals playing baseball. Was it possible for me to acquire Coach Ross's mental set, the expectations of an experienced scout? The introductory lecture went something like this:

Get to the park early. Watch batting practice. A boy – Coach Ross often referred to a "boy" rather than a "player" – *might walk four times in the game and a scout wouldn't see him swing. Watch the team take infield. You might not see him throw during a game.*

"There was a boy who played right field on a high school team. Wasn't a starter. Wasn't even a pitcher. Left-handed. When he threw before the game he air-mailed a toss over the third baseman's head into the bleachers, from deep right. He had a powerful arm. A scout saw him throw, saw the arm strength, wrote a report, and later drafted him. The boy ended up pitching in the big leagues."

If you're going to see a specific player, remember: you're scouting the player, not watching a game. Watch how he runs on and off the field, how he interacts with his coaches and teammates, whether he respects umpires. Watch the player's body language. You're scouting a body, but you're also scouting a whole person. You're scouting his character. Some things can be seen with the eye; other qualities have to be inferred from what you can see: determination and courage, drive and heart. They're more indirect.

The best professional baseball players are good athletes. Good ballplayers have great skills; skills are rooted in athleticism. Coaches can teach a kid to develop good baseball skills, but a coach can't teach him to be a good athlete. He either has It – a high degree of athleticism – or he doesn't. You can see the aliveness, the energy of a good athlete in the way he plays. Look for a wound-tight body. Dead bodies aren't prospects. Scouts evaluate youngsters who will grow and develop. Don't begin your evaluation with skills. In a young ballplayer a scout first looks for tools, natural talents. A scout may say of a boy: "He's toolsy." A scout can see tools. Don't worry so much about what a boy is now, whether he's a skilled player. If he has tools, don't worry about the present. Baseball scouts try to see the future. That's why scouting is so hard and why scouts make so many mistakes. Tom Greenwade saw Mickey's future; other scouts missed it.

Speed and arm strength are the most important tools for a position player. Not only can you see tools, you can measure some of them.

Speed is important for both offense and defense. The first thing scouts do at a tryout camp is to time players in the 60 yard dash, the distance from home to second on an extra base hit, or second to home on a single to the outfield. Always take your stopwatch to the ballpark. For a right-handed hitter: 4.2 seconds is the major league average to first base; 4.1 for a left-handed batter. But you must be careful. Some boys are slow out of the batter's box, or they take more time to get to full speed. Long striders might fool you because they don't seem as fast as short striders.

Speed isn't the same thing as quickness and range, especially for an infielder. Infielders need good feet, but range also requires anticipation, reading pitch location and swings. In the outfield pure speed is more important, as well as the instinct to get good jumps and take good angles to the ball. On the infield, having good hands, the ability to react quickly to the way the ball hops, is important. Speed and quickness are different factors for good infield and outfield play. And no thick legs for middle infielders. Scouts want skinny legs and small butts. If you see a boy at shortstop who has good hands, a strong arm, but thick legs, you might project him as a catcher in pro ball.

The other basic tool a scout can see is arm strength. You can see velocity for position players and pitchers. A scout can measure a catcher's arm strength: the time it takes to catch the ball and throw it to second base on a steal. It's called pop time. The average pop time for a major league catcher is 2.0 seconds. A catcher's pop time also involves how quickly he moves his feet and releases the ball. That's also a function of athleticism.

"I'm going to see a boy this summer from a small town southwest of Oklahoma City: Binger. He plays for the Anadarko American Legion team. He's a catcher and I heard someone timed him at 1.8 to second base. Great name: Johnny Bench. I don't know if the boy can play but if he has a 1.8 pop time I know he can throw. If he's an athlete and he throws like that, he's a prospect."

It's almost impossible to develop a good arm; it's a blessing, God-given, as Pastor Fred would say. Scouts want to see players who have been gifted, blessed with natural athletic talents. Scouts look for tools – professional skills come later.

Coach Ross talked about the "Five Tools" as if he was describing the core of a religious worldview: The Four Noble Truths, The Seven Deadly Sins, The Ten Commandments, The Trinity. The Five Tools are the five ways a position player can beat an opponent: speed, arm, fielding, hitting for average, hitting for power. There are few ballplayers, even in the big leagues, who can beat you in five ways – the great ones can. Why did Mickey Mantle become one of the greatest players of all time? He's a five-tool player.

"When I first played against Mickey, I could see the speed, the arm, the power. God-given. Blessed. The Yankees found the right place to take advantage of his speed and arm and he became a fine outfielder. His ability to hit for average in professional baseball was immediately obvious the first season after he signed. Here's a story about his speed – hard to believe. Somebody timed Mickey in 3.2 to first base, on a drag bunt from the left-side, so he had a running start. How is that even possible?"

In some ways it's easier to scout pitchers than position players, because a scout can see velocity, as well as the movement of a pitcher's fast ball. When scouting a pitcher always sit behind home plate. Is his fast ball straight or does it have life? Does it have run? Does it sink? Is there some deceptiveness in a pitcher's delivery? Does the ball seem to get on the hitter quickly? Does the pitcher have a smooth, repeatable delivery? If he's herky-jerky, does it affect his control? Scouts want to see a curve ball with good bite, strong rotation, north to south tilt, sliders with snap, a deceptive difference in speed between a pitcher's fastball and his change-of-speed pitches.

In a pitcher, look for athleticism, length, and minimum effort. That's why scouts stay away from "little righties," short armers, and pitchers who strain on each pitch. Less effort and good mechanics mean fewer arm injuries, better control, and more innings.

"I'm looking for a boy who's tall and lean, with a good body, smooth delivery, high ¾ release point, strides straight to the plate, throws hard, good control, commands the strike zone with at least two pitches, misses and breaks bats with a fastball that had good life…and loves to have the ball in his hand. Confident. A competitor. A little nasty. Hungry. Fearless."

On my first scouting trip we drove to Shattuck, Oklahoma, near the Texas border, about thirty miles southwest of Woodward. Pastor Fred chaperoned; he was also interested in Coach Ross's part-time gig, who was there to scout a player from another tiny town in northwest Oklahoma, not Shattuck, smaller than Conway. We pulled up to a wonderful old ballpark: faded green grandstand, advertisements painted on the outfield fences, manicured grass, precise edges, deep rusty infield dirt. Somebody in Shattuck cared.

Coach Ross glowed with appreciation. "It reminds me of ballparks I played in – in the old K-O-M Class D league."

Coach Ross decided not to tell us which player he was scouting. It was my first test. There was no batting practice. We watched players warm up in the outfield. We watched both teams take infield. There was no position player on Shattuck's team who stood out. Then Kiowa ran on the field. It was obvious who Coach Ross was scouting. I turned to him.

"It's the shortstop, isn't it?"

"That's right. And I'm not alone. See that guy over there, in the fishing hat? That's Bert Wells. He's the head Midwest scout for the Dodgers."

Coach Ross had explained the 20-80 scale he used to evaluate tools. "50" means that the player has a major league average tool. That was a big problem for me. I could see a young player's tools compared to other players on the field or other players I had seen. But Coach Ross was using a different mental set. His standard of comparison was an ideal, a concept in his mind, an image of a type: a major league player. He was working from a stereotype, a pattern which he could apply to individual players. I called it a schema, a basis for generating a standard of comparison between what he sees and what he's looking for. If I wanted to be a scout I would have to see more professional games; I would have to be able to develop an effective schema for evaluation. I needed to see particular examples of an ideal type. If 50 was major league average speed, arm, and power, were Mickey's tools 70s? Was his power an 80? Was Lou Brock's speed a 70?

A scout's shorthand evaluation for above-major-league average was to call it a "plus" tool. If a pitcher has a plus fastball, it's a pitch that's better than an average major leaguer's. Coach Ross's scale and evaluation were attempts to communicate what he saw and the judgments he made about his observations, against the background of a concept of the ideal.

That day in Shattuck it was obvious that Kiowa's shortstop was the best player on the field, but how good was he when compared to professional players? How good was he going to be? A scouting report typically contains an evaluation of current tools, as well as a projection of the future. An eighteen year old high school star might have 40 power, but his body might be projected to develop, fill out, and turn into a 50 tool.

Here's coach Ross's report on the Kiowa shortstop:

Six feet, 175 pounds. Wound-tight body. Average speed and arm. Soft hands and clean action. Good bat speed and habits at the plate. Quiet bat. Mature sense of the strike zone – doesn't chase. Stays back. Short stride. Loose hands. Short stroke. Doesn't get fooled by off-speed pitches. Hunts a good pitch to hit. Uses the whole field. Can turn on inside pitch and take the outside pitch the other way. Good two-strike approach. Has a knack for hitting the ball on the barrel. Good face. A nice looking boy.

I asked Coach Ross about his final descriptions. "A good face? What do you mean by a "good face"?

"Well, it's hard to explain. It's not quite literal but it is kind of literal. You're around players and ballparks all the time, and sometimes you can just pick out the best player because he looks the part. You see determination, confidence, strength, the shine of excellence. That kid from Kiowa – he looks like an All-American. He has the prettiest girlfriend, the nicest, hardest-working parents – all-everything at each point in his life, the expectations of greatness. He's solid in his skin. Everyone looks up to him. He radiates success. He has a good face."

"What about the numbers?

"He already has a 50 arm, 50 speed, maybe 45 power – I'd project him to have average power when he matures. 45 hitter – he'll be 50. He'll be a 50 middle infielder, maybe a plus infielder."

"So you're saying he has at least two major league tools now, in high school?"

"That's right."

"Right here, from Kiowa, small town northwest Oklahoma, population nothing?"

"It happens. Think about Mickey Mantle."

"Do you think he'll be drafted? Will he play in the big leagues?"

"If he doesn't get hurt, develops, and gets in the right organization, I think he'll play in the big leagues. He'll go in the top five rounds of the draft. He signed with Oklahoma State, so if the money isn't right, he'll go to college. He's definitely a good prospect."

In June 1967, the Kiowa shortstop was drafted in the second round by the Yankees. He didn't sign. Went to OSU. All-American. Drafted again, by the Twins. He made his major league debut five years after we saw him in Shattuck.

I became an apprentice scout. In late spring Coach Ross's crew drove to Stillwater to see Oklahoma State play the University of Oklahoma. I asked questions. Is that a 50 arm in centerfield? "Not quite. He might have a chance in left. Strongest arm and best power usually in right. Best athlete in center. Shortest arm in left."

I liked an OU skinny lefthander with a weird arm angle. He looked like he was pushing the ball, but he baffled the OSU hitters. The catcher's mitt popped with a good fastball. I asked Coach Ross about him. "I worry a little about his mechanics and his stature, but he has nice life on his fastball. The curve sweeps, not much bite, but that can be corrected. He'll be a draft."

"How high?"

"I'd say somewhere in the tenth to twentieth round."

I followed the progress of players we evaluated. The OU skinny lefthander made it to Triple A with the San Francisco Giants, but he didn't pitch in the big leagues.

We attended a GPSC game in Alma, against one of the directional state colleges: Southwestern State College, Weatherford, Oklahoma. Coach Ross wanted to see a Southwestern pitcher, a tall, long, lean Black kid, low ¾ delivery, with a nice sinking fastball.

"I don't know how the big schools missed on this kid. Probably because he came from a small school down in the far southwest corner of Oklahoma, west of Altus: Gould. He's going to fill out, throw harder. Wicky fastball. Must throw it with two seams. Good movement. A nice little slider. I like him."

The pitcher from Southwestern had a nice major league career and an even longer career as a professional pitching coach. I was learning.

We left Conway early Monday morning. The drive to St. Louis was nine hours; we wanted to be in Busch Stadium for the first pitch: game one of a four-game series with the Cincinnati Reds. Pastor Fred scheduled our summer baseball trip after wheat harvest, after the first cycle of working the fields, turning under the stubble, between Sunday sermons and appropriately placed to take advantage of Tuesday's Fourth of July celebration at the ballpark. We would be in St. Louis for the entire four game series, then see a Triple A game in Tulsa on Friday night on our way back to Conway – I insisted. Jean would be baseball-bored for only five days.

Although I had been to many games in St. Louis over a number of years, the experience was new, stimulating in a fresh way. I was there to scout tools, not simply to see a game. I could now give some specific content to a mental set defined quantitatively, abstractly located in high school and college ballparks, fully actualized in Busch Stadium, where average tools were embodied in a more understandable network of comparisons. Abstract seeing became more concrete. My scouting schema became less vague, more defined, a concept no longer in search of a particular.

In those games, brilliant tools were apparent: Lou Brock's speed; Orlando Cepeda's power; Curt Flood's outfield jumps; Julian Javier's hands; Tim McCarver's deft handling of Bob Gibson's plus fastball; and diminutive shortstop Dal Maxvill, showing scouts that you could be a fine major league middle infielder without two (and perhaps three) of the five tools: he couldn't hit very well, and he had no power.

Three Cincinnati Reds players stood out: Vada Pinson and Pete Rose, both ordinary size, 5'11". Rose was stockier, full of energy, wound-tight (as Scout Ross would say), scrappy, slashing hits around the ballpark; Pinson was a beautiful player, graceful at the plate and in centerfield. And big Tony Perez had plus power, like Cepeda, and a joy of playing, like Pete Rose. Right fielder Art Shamsky had a plus arm.

For two games we sat behind home plate so I could better scout the pitchers. Milt Pappas and Jim Maloney threw hard, but not like Gibson. Reds pitcher Gary Nolan showed me a plus curve ball in a 3-hit, nine inning shutout of the Cardinals. I was surprised that a left-handed, soft tossing reliever for the Cards had made it to the big leagues. And I was convinced that the young high school shortstop from Kiowa would be a better player than Dal Maxvill.

On Friday night we were in Tulsa, Oklahoma, to see the Tulsa Oilers play in Oiler Park, Pacific Coast League, Triple A affiliate of the Cardinals. We were there to scout minor league players, some of whom would make The Show: Coco Laboy, Elio Chacon, Mike Torrez, Tracy Stallard, Nick Wilhite.

The starting pitcher for the Oilers was an eighteen year old kid who had been the Cardinal's second round pick in the 1967 draft. He was tall, at least 6'4", probably 190 pounds, threw hard, and got shelled. I never found out what the parent club had in mind, throwing a kid into the highest level of minor league baseball right after high school. His name was Jerry Reuss (ROYCE). Two years later, at age 20, he made his major league debut with the Cardinals. He played with a number of different teams and lasted until 1990, aged 41. He won 220 games in the major leagues. I watched him carefully. He reminded me of someone I knew. That night, I couldn't see the future.

In the story I told to myself, the summer trip with Pastor Fred was special. I felt we were growing apart. His sermons fell flat. His passions were no longer wholly mine: Jesus Christ and the St. Louis Cardinals. At least we still had the Cardinals. We kept score and scouted together. He seemed to enjoy evaluating players' tools as much as I did. We could still share games on the radio and we could see and imagine baseball events as father and daughter. We could feel the tribal joy of the Cardinals beating the Red Sox in the World Series that fall. But I wasn't sure that baseball would be enough to bind us closely into our future. His absolute ground was religious and biblical. I found myself slipping, perhaps a natural but momentary youthful imbalance. I wanted to talk to him about serious things but I couldn't. My senior year, my momentous year, would complete The Fall.

I also tried to talk to Jake about serious things, but he was uninterested, a house with a locked door – a mind without the kind of furniture that was welcoming to my thinking. He was bright yet incurious about topics I found puzzling or confusing.

I tried to explain to him my thinking about God and the death of little Sarah.

"Jake, it's perfectly logical. If God is all-powerful he can do anything. If God knows everything, then he knew about Sarah's illness and suffering. If God loves us, with a love that is so great we can't understand its greatness – as Pastor Fred says – then he loved Sarah and cared for her – at least as much as we did. But Sarah suffered and died. So something doesn't make sense. Either God couldn't help Sarah, or didn't know about her illness, or he didn't care about her. Or, maybe He's not there."

"Lizzie, you have your head in the clouds. Where do you come up with this stuff?"

"I don't know. What do you think? Maybe God isn't what we believe Him to be. Or, maybe he doesn't exist."

"Lizzie, you're a preacher's kid. How can you even think that? You're asking questions that can't be answered. No one knows what God is like."

"Pastor Fred claims to know a lot about God: why He does things; how and why He created us; why He sent his Son to save us from our sins, because He loves us so much. Well, if He loves us so much how do we explain Sarah's death?"

"He took her to Heaven, I guess."

"But what about her suffering? Even if she's in Heaven, why did she have to suffer – and die so young?"

"Your dad says we have to have faith in God's will. We have to believe."

"But why? Why do we have to believe? Why do we need faith?"

"We just do."

"That no answer. Why do we have to have faith? Because we have to have faith."

"We need faith so we can go to Heaven."

"That still doesn't make it right when children suffer. Is it worth it?"

"I don't know, Lizzie. Let's talk about something else."

On another occasion he did wonder – about one of his classmates.

"Do you think Phil is a queer?" I had heard some of Jake's friends call him "Phyllis."

"Queer?"

"Yeah, Queer. You know – he likes guys better than girls."

"I don't know. I never really thought about it."

"Don't you think it's a little weird that he's a cheerleader? He acts like a girl."

"So what if he does? Why does it matter?"

"Don't you think it's wrong? Doesn't the Bible say it's wrong?"

"If someone likes someone else, whether it's a boy or a girl, and he's not hurting anyone, I don't see the problem. I think he can live however he wants."

"Wow, Lizzie. You're out there sometimes."

We were on firmer ground when we talked about baseball. I explained what I was learning about scouting. He thought my lessons were very interesting and wondered how scouts would evaluate his pro prospects.

"You have good hands and feet, and you're quick. Scouts would like that. You might be a 50 infielder."

"How do I compare with the Kiowa shortstop?"

Not favorably, I thought. I didn't have the heart to tell him he didn't look much like the Kiowa shortstop. "He's bigger and faster and he has a stronger arm and more power, but you can hit for average. And you're a switch-hitter. That's positive. You might have to switch to second base in pro ball. It all depends on how you develop."

He was optimistic about his pro prospects. I wasn't. I didn't think my boyfriend was a pro prospect, but I thought he could be a good college player.

"The Littles asked me to go with them on their trip to New York. They're going to pay for me, and my parents gave me permission to go."

"Why do you want to go to New York?"

"Big cities are exciting! We're going to do all sorts of stuff: museums, a play, music. And Dr. Little likes baseball. He's going to get us tickets to a Yankees game. We're going to see Mickey Mantle play!"

"*That's* a reason to go to New York!"

In late summer, 1967, I traveled to an alternate universe, far from the provinces of the Great Plains. There are moments that are always with me.

The hotel room I share with Marcia Little is near Fifty-Fourth and Seventh Avenue. I look down toward Seventh Avenue and see Stage Delicatessen, where Mickey Mantle was a regular in 1951, just arrived from Commerce, Oklahoma, a ballplaying hick hobnobbing with celebrities, beautiful people, and mobsters. He two-timed his girlfriend back home and took up with a young actress who was as impressed with a handsome and muscular young Yankee as he was with a divorced beauty queen. He later shared an apartment above the deli – right down there – with teammates; he slept on a cot in the living room. Dr. and Mrs. Little, Marcia, and I have sandwiches in the deli. I imagine Mickey sitting at a big table, the center of attention, holding court after a big day at the ballpark – big smile, free food, on top of the world, future star of the Bronx Bombers.

We take a cab downtown, stroll through New York University, where my Jim Burden-like fantasies get the best of me. Is that a coffee house where Dylan played? We eat in Greenwich Village. We have tickets to "Man of La Mancha," playing at Washington Square Theatre. My cultural host, Marcia's father, the good physician, provides the background explanations for a play within a play. Cervantes or Don Quixote? That fall I borrowed Mrs. Wilson's copy of *Don Quixote* and spent weeks amused and disturbed by Quixote's strange chivalrous delusions.

A concert in Central Park. A day in The Metropolitan Museum of Art. The weird world of The Museum of Modern Art. Then – a religious experience.

We emerge from underground, the subway train modestly crowded for a Sunday afternoon game at Yankee Stadium. The concierge said tickets would be no problem. The Yankees weren't very good in the summer of 1967; most of the stars from the early 60's were gone: Maris, Skowron, Richardson, Kubek, Boyer, Lopez, Howard. The current roster consisted of forgettable, no-name players – except for the Great One, a fading Mickey Mantle playing in his next to last season. The Yankees would finish eighteen games below .500, in ninth place in the American League.

We emerged from darkness into light. The tracks are elevated, beyond the centerfield fence, giving us a first birds-eye view of Yankee Stadium, sitting splendidly in an ocean of buildings, inhabited by the spirits of other Great Ones, whose deeds are as much a part of this sacred space as fallen heroes dwelling on a famous battlefield. My first view of the stadium left me with a sense of the sublime. I knew the history. I had been in other major league ballparks, in St. Louis and Kansas City, but I had never been in the ultimate baseball cathedral. The white decorative façade, looming from atop the third deck, dented one day by one of Mickey's impossible home runs. The monuments to greatness in centerfield. The quirky dimensions: they giveth and they taketh away. Pint-sized homeruns, hit toward the short porch in right field. One of Mickey's 450 foot lift-offs, towering above the lights, becomes a warning-track out in deep left center.

The Yankees beat the Minnesota Twins that day, 7-3. The Twins were good, much better than the Yankees. Tony Oliva hit two homeruns, each landing a few rows up in right field. Harmon Killebrew, the "Killer," had a hit. A former MVP, Zoilo Versalles, played shortstop, Jim Perry, Gaylord's brother, pitched. For the Yankees, Mel Stottlemyre was the winning pitcher, and an unusual interloper, Joe Pepitone, played in the hallowed spot that should have been taken by Mickey Mantle. I appreciated them all, but at this dance I have eyes for only one partner: number 7, who plays first base and runs with a slight limp. My task was to see the past rather than the present or the future. He couldn't run well but the swing was still holy. He had a double and knocked in two runs. I see the Myth in the man and I'm ready to return to Conway.

The wheat harvest was terrible that year. The pulsing energy of my first harvest was missing. There were fewer trucks and combines clogging the dirt roads and Conway's streets. The lines of trucks to the grain elevator were shorter. There had been drought conditions for most of the fall and winter months; a late freeze retarded wheat growth even further. The heads of the plants refused to fill out. Instead of an over-crowded sea of waving, fuzzy-headed, bright fields, the land was thinly populated by stunted shoots that would deliver a meager crop. Some fields made only ten bushels per acre; in other fields, farmers didn't bother to cut the wheat. They plowed under the scrawny plants because the crop wasn't worth the cost of cutting and delivery to the Co-op.

It would be a lean year for farmers with smaller acreages and tenuous mortgages. The Kirchners were hurting because of Sarah's death. Now God or Nature (as Spinoza described Ultimate Reality) piled on. John took a part-time job in Alma. Virginia cleaned houses in Conway. The Methodist preacher complained about lighter collection plates on Sunday and Conway merchants felt the pain. Prayers were more pointed and meteorological; farmers became petitioners asking God for rain rather than forgiveness.

At Conway High School there was, among some of my classmates, senior-year optimism to puncture community gloom. For us the future was wide open and full of promise. Marcia was going to apply to the University of Oklahoma and Jake was pretty sure he was going to play baseball at Great Plains State College. Alma had started an American Legion team and he was the starting shortstop, leading hitter, and best player. GPSC's head coach had talked to him and a scholarship offer would probably be forthcoming at some point in Jake's senior year.

I was happy for Jake because I knew how much he loved baseball and how much the Dream was still alive – he wanted to be paid to play. I couldn't help but feel a little envy and a sense of unfairness in the way the institutions of sports allowed Jake to have opportunities to pursue his athletic dreams while I (as well as other girls) was left behind.

Title IX proclaimed: "No person in the United States shall, on the basis of sex, be excluded from participation in, or denied the benefits of, or subjected to discrimination under any educational program or activity receiving financial aid." That law included all aspects of education, including opportunities to play sports, because most school districts, colleges, and universities received funds from the federal government. Thus, after 1972, most high school and college sports were governed by Title IX, which required equal opportunities for female and male athletes. I had the misfortune of playing before the revolution.

Would it have mattered? Was I good enough to play college sports, ignoring for the moment that I didn't even get the chance to play high school softball? According to one experienced judge, the answer was "yes."

His name was Dale Parker, but everyone called him "Coach" Parker. I met him one day in downtown Conway. I knew who he was because I had seen him many, many times at practices and games. He attended almost all of Conway High School sporting events. He stood in the corner, court-level, for my basketball games. He sometimes showed up at practices, acknowledged by Coach Ross and Mr. Hadwiger, the boys basketball coach. He was there when Coach Ross let me participate in baseball practices: shagging flies, taking batting practice and infield, participating in drills and running races. He was there when Mr. Hadwiger asked me to practice with the boys basketball team, to help the second team be more challenging for the first team by running an upcoming opponent's offense, especially if the opponent had an effective point guard. He was often at my summer softball games in Alma. He showed up in Enid at a big tournament with teams competing from around the state. Our all-star team from Alma finished third and I was named to the All-Tournament team.

He walked up to me, reached out his hand, smiled warmly, and introduced himself. "I'm Dale Parker. Everybody calls me Coach Parker."

Coach Parker had graduated from Conway High and played basketball and baseball at Great Plains State College, in "prehistoric times," he said, before the war. He taught and coached at Conway for over twenty years: social studies, baseball, boys and girls basketball. People said he was a fine coach: intense, often impatient, competitive, strategic, tough, but fair and loving. He finally had enough of parent complaints and small-town politics. He quit teaching and coaching, farmed a quarter section somewhere between Conway and Alma, took a job with the post office delivering mail – but never stopped loving sports and the kids who played them.

I guessed he was in his mid to late sixties. He looked fit and athletic. Scout Ross might have said he still looked "wound-tight." Over six feet tall, thick without being fat, prominent brown biceps and arms, big neck, deep crevices in his tanned face, large leathery hands. When we shook hands his grip was imposing – I'm sure he was holding back.

"I'm Lizzie Ware. Nice to meet you Coach Parker."

"I know who you are. I've been watching you since you arrived in Conway as a ninth grader. I wish I could have had an athlete like you when I coached. Actually, I wish I could have coached you."

"I've seen you at my games and practices. You must be a big sports fan."

"I am, Lizzie. I love sports. Been around sports my whole life. I've seen most of the players who have come out of these parts, for over forty years – girls as well as boys. I've gone to most of the state tournaments through the years. And I wanted to tell you something."

He looked into my eyes. He now looked so serious. I had just met him.

"Lizzie Ware, it has been one of the pleasures of my life to watch you grow and develop and become what you are. You are not only the best athlete ever to come out of Conway; you're one of the best ever to come out of northwest Oklahoma, maybe the whole state of Oklahoma."

"Thank you, Coach Parker. Thank you very much."

"I also wanted to tell you that I still have quite a few contacts. Would you like to keep playing after high school?"

"Yes, of course!"

"Maybe AAU ball?"

"What's that?"

We chatted for a few minutes. I now had an agent.

"I'll see what I can do. Good luck in your senior year. We'll be talking."

My relationship with Jake was developing along other lines. I didn't think I was merely an infatuated teenager consumed by a first love. I was mature enough, I thought, to distinguish a rhinestone and a gem.

One Saturday night we went parking. That is, *Parking* – in the country, in the dark, a few miles from Alma, on a dirt road where the situation afforded us the privacy to explore each other in more intimate ways. Pastor Fred and Jean thought we were playing cards in Alma with Marcia and her Almatian boyfriend, at his house – which we did. But we left early.

We drove south from Alma, toward Conway for a few miles. Jake turned west.

"Where are we going?" I knew what he had in mind but I thought I should appear surprised. We had been working – not working but playing – toward this moment for some time. Marcia had asked me whether we had gone "parking," among the wheat fields, with the ultimate end a possibility – but for me it would lead to no-play or no-end. Strictly front seat, no back seat play. It was another marker for us, and one I gladly embraced.

Did I have any Methodist guilt as our physical relationship advanced? No, not at all. I loved Jake and he loved me. I was sure we had a future, despite our differences. But it did make things more complicated if our college paths diverged. I was confident that we would be together forever.

The campus of Great Plains State College sits in the south part of Alma on a hill – at least it sits on the highest spot in town, almost a hill. It is located a few blocks from the town square, at the end of College Street, which rises gently to a plateau accommodating a cluster of brick buildings, mature leafy elms and oaks and locust trees, green open spaces, and late summer colors in beds and bushes. It's a refreshing oasis in the expanse of outlying brownness.

I could see why the founders chose this spot for a fledgling land grant college, in 1897. It was an apt living metaphor for higher education, emerging from the uncultured, uncivilized flatness that surrounded the campus. Alma had appeared overnight, September 16, 1893, the day of the Cherokee Outlet (Strip) Land Run. The townsite was conveniently located near the railroad running southwest from the Kansas border where the run originated. Alma was designated as a location for filing a claim. Survive the chaos of the start, find the surveyor's stone marker on the corner of a prized quarter section, drive a stake into the ground, and rush to Alma – which only recently had come into being – to seal a claim on the future.

It's late afternoon. Classes began on Tuesday, the day after Labor Day. I'm here on Thursday, to sit in on a twice-a-week, late afternoon course: Philosophy 101: Introduction to Philosophy, taught by Professor Enos Taylor. I drove here in the family car to attend the first lecture, on the nature and fields of philosophy, to be followed by classes throughout the semester in which the professor instructs more in the manner of Socrates than a sage on a stage. I won't attend every class; I have my Conway High responsibilities, which will include Mrs. Wilson's taxing journey through English literature. But I have been Called…and I have responded. Professor Taylor's invitation to sit in on the class, to be introduced to the study of philosophy, seemed irresistible, despite my ignorance of what I would be studying.

Philosophy. It sounded mysterious and important, grown-up, intellectually sophisticated. Would we be looking for the meaning of life?

He sent the syllabus in late summer. Mrs. Wilson loaned her books to me. No textbook – just primary texts written by great philosophers:

Euthyphro, Apology, Crito, Plato

Proslogion, Anselm

"The Five Ways," Aquinas

Meditations on First Philosophy, Descartes

An Inquiry Concerning Human Understanding, Hume

On Liberty, J. S. Mill

Existentialism from Dostoevsky to Sartre, Kaufmann, editor

I had heard of Plato. I had never heard of the other philosophers we would read. I had heard of "existentialism;" Mrs. Wilson may have made some comments about it. It sounded exotic, deep, profound. But what does the term mean? There were ten authors in the text on existentialism, including four writers of fiction (Dostoevsky, Kafka, Sartre, and Camus) and a poet (Rilke). There were atheists and theists. There were German, French, Danish, and Spanish philosophers. There were both nineteenth and twentieth century writers and thinkers.

Paster Fred and Jean had no idea what I was studying with Professor Taylor. I overheard my father telling someone at church that I was taking a psychology course at the college. He was wrong on two counts: I wasn't enrolled in the course and he misunderstood the two disciplines. I wasn't being introduced to a college-level study of a social science. I was being introduced to a different kind of thinking, about the most fundamental questions a reflective human being might raise. Some were questions which Pastor Fred had answered long ago, with the help of a community of believers and infallible appeals to biblical authority. There were no such appeals in philosophy. According to Professor Taylor there was no authority other than our own rational minds attempting to answer important questions for ourselves.

Our first reading assignment was the *Euthyphro*, a dialogue written by Plato, an ancient Greek philosopher. I read it twice before class. I wasn't sure how to read it. It was a conversation between Socrates and Euthyphro, a piece of philosophical fiction, although Socrates was a real, historical person who engaged in the kind of activity portrayed in the dialogue: question, answer, discussion, argument, criticism, and more questions. Socrates was clever, quick with examples and analogies. Euthyphro seemed familiar to me. He was some kind of priest who claimed to have expert knowledge in religious matters. Was he an ancient version of my father?

Professor Taylor was friendly, non-threatening, engaging, even enthusiastic. He asked questions and made comments: "Interesting." "Okay!" "Why do you say that?" He wrote our answers on the chalkboard. He referred to passages in the text. He asked us to defend our answers by referring to the text, or he encouraged us to interpret some passage. "What is Socrates arguing in this paragraph?" He wanted to appear to be jointly engaged with us in a fresh inquiry, as if he was interrogating the text for the first time. He was leading us somewhere, without appearing to lead us – like Socrates in the dialogue. I wasn't sure what to look for, until Professor Taylor started asking us questions which were simultaneously clarifying and often puzzling. Our discussion soon mirrored the dialogue. We were doing philosophy.

Professor Taylor began by asking us to describe the situation in which the conversation takes place and the characters. (I intended to remain silent.) They meet near a court. Euthyphro is there to prosecute his father for the murder of a murderer, which occurred in questionable circumstances. His family believes it is the height of impiety for a son to accuse his father of murder. Euthyphro, however, is utterly certain he is acting piously, that is, rightly. He thinks the Gods are on his side. Socrates is at the court for his own trial, charged with impious conduct: religious innovation and corrupting Athenian youth. Socrates is puzzled. He raises the fundamental question in the dialogue: What is piety? A more modern way to raise the issue: what is morally right conduct? What makes a morally right act right? Socrates invites Euthyphro to become his teacher, since Euthyphro must know what piety is, or else he wouldn't be prosecuting his father. Teach me, says Socrates. It will help me in my own trial. I'm eager to become your pupil. Before long, the irony is obvious.

Euthyphro is boastful, pretentious, arrogant, dogmatic, unreflective, shallow, and vain. Socrates is intellectually humble, careful, reflective, a quick thinker, a lover of truth. Euthyphro is a dogmatic fool – Socrates is a philosopher. Professor Taylor asks us to keep in mind an overriding question: What is Plato trying to show us?

Surely, I thought, Plato was trying to show us what it means to be a philosopher. He was depicting the difference between two kinds of people and recommending that we should be more like Socrates. We should not claim to know what we do not know. Wisdom is recognizing one's ignorance, so the desire to inquire can flourish. Socrates claimed that the unexamined life is not worth living – it is no life for a human being to live. Our distinctiveness resides in our capacity to reason. And Socrates was teaching Euthyphro to confront his own ignorance, his philosophical limitations.

I was captivated. Socrates was Plato's philosophical hero; Plato's hero also became mine. I wanted to be like Socrates, a lover of wisdom devoted to seeking truth about important questions.

Some students didn't like Socrates. They thought he was an obnoxious smart aleck, badgering Euthyphro, trying to make him look bad. I raised my hand. It's Euthyphro who takes Socrates' ironic bait, I said. Euthyphro is the one who claims to know the nature of pious action. I referred to the text. He says, "I should be of no use, Socrates, and Euthyphro would not be superior to the majority of men, if I did not have accurate knowledge of all such things." Professor Taylor smiled.

What is Plato trying to show us? Does Socrates think there is an answer to the question? A consensus seemed to be forming among students: Plato is showing the reader there are no true answers to philosophical questions, since no successful definition of piety is found. There's really no truth other than what one believes to be true. Everyone has their (sic) own opinion. Truth is subjective. Socrates and Euthyphro are simply sharing their views with one another. What's true for me isn't necessarily true for you. The verbal members of class were student relativists.

I raised my hand again. "That's not at all what Plato is trying to show us," I said. He's showing us how difficult philosophical questions are and that we must think hard and carefully when trying to answer them. But...what would be the point of the dialogue if Socrates really thinks there's no answer to be found? And at one point in the text, he says as much, when Socrates says to Euthyphro, "...you are not keen to teach me, that's clear. You were on the point of doing so, but you turned away. If you had given that answer, I should now have acquired from you sufficient knowledge of the nature of piety. As it is, the lover of inquiry must follow his beloved wherever it may lead him." And at the end of the dialogue, just before Euthyphro abruptly leaves in frustration, Socrates is ready to begin again, because he is convinced the issue is fundamentally important and there is truth to be found.

Professor Taylor asks me to read Socrates' final speech:

What a thing to do, my friend. By going you have cast me down from a great hope I had. That I would learn from you the nature of the pious and the impious and so escape Meletus' (Socrates' accuser) indictment by showing him that I had acquired wisdom in divine matters from Euthyphro, and my ignorance would no longer cause me to be careless and inventive about such things, and that I would be better for the rest of my life.

Professor Taylor suggests that the dialogue's central theme is about the foundation of morality. What makes an act morally right? Euthyphro's answer: Piety is what all the Gods love. Piety is what is dear or pleasing to the Gods. The property that makes an act right is the Gods' attitudes towards it. His view is expressed in the monotheistic Divine Command Theory: an act is morally right if and only if it is commanded by God; an act is morally wrong if it is prohibited by God. The foundation of morality is religious. That sounded familiar to me, since Pastor Fred preached that we know what is right only through God and there could be no morality without God proclaiming His divine rules in the Bible, in the Ten Commandments. In a godless world, everything is permitted.

Enter Socrates with his famous question. Do the Gods love the pious because it is pious, or is it pious because the Gods love it? Professor Taylor: "Do you see the implications of Socrates question? For us?" Is conduct right just because God commands it, or does God command it because it's right? Does God make an action right just by commanding it, and wrong just by prohibiting it? Or does He, like us, recognize what is right?

"Can anyone explain the implications of Socrates' question for the foundation of morality? For what makes a morally right act right?" No one spoke. I waited, then raised my hand.

A noted British philosopher once said that "one good test of a person's aptitude for philosophy is to discover whether he can grasp (the) force and point" of the Euthyphro question, translated into the language of monotheism. I passed the test. I grasped the point: unless God commands right actions because they are right (be kind, act justly, don't murder or rob, keep your promises) then He could, in principle, make anything right, just by commanding. "Eat babies on Tuesday!" That would be arbitrary. It was also completely mysterious how God's commands could make an action right or wrong. There must be something about an action, whether it harms or treats someone unfairly, for example, that makes acts right or wrong. The reason Sarah's death was so tragic is that it deprived her of life, with all of its goods. Whether God desired it in his Grand Plan was irrelevant. Independent of God's commands or prohibitions, child abuse is wrong because it harms a child. Socrates agreed. If there is a God (or there are Gods), He must command right actions because they are right; their rightness is independent of God. As Harry said, we don't need God or religion to be good and we don't need God or religion for there to *be* good.

I left the class that day with a feeling of excitement, and the sense that philosophical thinking was natural for me. I talked to other students in class. Many found philosophy impractical, useless, hopelessly abstract and distant from "real life." I didn't understand why they couldn't see the importance of learning to think for oneself instead of simply believing what we are taught or what is available in our society. I began to see the truth in a quote from Bertrand Russell, which Professor Taylor shared with us in the first lecture. "...the man who has no tincture of philosophy goes through life imprisoned in the prejudices derived from common sense, from the habitual beliefs of his age or his nation, and from convictions which have grown up in his mind without the cooperation or consent of his deliberate reason."

My mind, which found itself spinning philosophical webs in my long walks in town and through the country and in my bedroom late at night after reading Whitman or Eliot or Cervantes, found its new home in Professor Taylor's classroom, and in the texts that challenged me to think in new ways.

I'm sitting in Professor Taylor's office after class. The days are getting shorter, the late afternoon shadows are thickening, and the wheat has been planted. I often talk with my teacher before class, during office hours, or for a few minutes after class. The crammed bookshelves make the room feel like a small cavern; the tall windows in this old building have little light to offer in late afternoon. We sit in the growing dusk, without the glare of overhead lights. A reflective and calming atmosphere. He fills in gaps for a class I've missed – and I have more questions.

Our class has made its way through (failed) medieval attempts to prove the existence of God, Descartes' fathering of modern philosophy, and to Hume's empiricism. I have acquired a new, Buddhist conception of the self: a bundle of fleeting impressions rather than a soul, Descartes' notion of an immaterial substance. Hume's empiricism is more persuasive than Descartes' rationalism. I have become a skeptic, an imitation of Hume, although Professor Taylor's beautiful lecture on Kant made me question Hume's account of causation. Next week we're moving to social and political philosophy: Mill's defense of classical liberalism and the Harm Principle. After that, we'll read Kierkegaard and Nietzsche, Sartre and Camus. I'll be an existentialist by the end of the term. I sometimes write short essays for my tutor, who corrects my writing, helps sharpen my arguments, and encourages me to dig deeper. In the world of philosophy, he's a coach and scout – and I'm a prospect.

Professor Taylor has taken a personal interest in me, probably because I have taken a personal interest in philosophy. We talk about the class, about the ideas and arguments we have been examining, but he also asks questions about me.

"Do you want to go to college?"

"Yes, of course."

"Have you thought about where you might go?"

"Probably here, GPSC, but I'd like to find a place to play basketball."

"Do you have any idea what you might want to major in?"

"Yes, I think I'll major in English. I'd like to be a high school teacher, like Mrs. Wilson."

"She's a wonderful teacher, isn't she? She was a fine student. So interested, so passionate about ideas. She was the best student I've ever had. She talked about pursuing graduate work in philosophy, but that didn't work out."

"Professor Taylor, how did you become interested in philosophy?"

He paused, looked away toward the window, then back at me. He smiled.

"It's not that interesting."

"I'd like to know. Was philosophy natural for you? Did you start asking questions when you were my age?"

"Yes, but I had no outlet, no one to talk to. I didn't know anything about philosophy, but I knew that I had questions, big questions."

"About religion? About God?"

"Yes, surely those were important for me."

"And you grew up here?"

"I grew up on a farm north of Alma and went to Alma High School. Before the war I was flailing, not sure what I wanted to do. I took math and science classes here at GPSC. I thought I might be a high school teacher. I joined the Navy after Pearl Harbor and was stationed in the South Pacific and took part in many battles. We had close calls by the dozens. We lived from day to day with the specter of death constantly hovering over us. I saw ships go down all around us; saw shipmates of my own take the mortal plunge into the sea as the Captain read a few unintelligible words over the flag-draped body as it was consigned to the deep. A rushed ceremony, so we could get back to the grim business of trying to kill someone else before we were attacked again."

The room was almost dark and Professor Taylor spoke quietly.

"One night our ship exchanged places with another destroyer, which was sunk and lost most of her men. My ship didn't get a scratch or lose a man. If we would have been in our original position I would have been killed. Was it luck? Blind contingency? Or is there some hidden, underlying Plan or some unseen, mechanical necessity in the unfolding events of the universe? I was haunted by these questions."

"My father says that all things happen according to God's will – God's plan. Do you believe that?"

"I don't know, Lizzie. What do you think?"

"I'm not sure. One of my friends, a little ten year-old girl suffered and died. I don't see how children suffering could ever be a part of God's plan."

"The suffering of children. It was the way that Dostoyevsky pointedly expressed the Problem of Evil in *The Brothers Karamazov*. He described shocking real-life examples of the suffering of children that no end or purpose could possibly justify. Have you read *Karamazov*?"

"No, but I will."

"I suppose war does something to most people who take part in combat. You can't help but think about big questions. God. Suffering. Death. Human nature. Politics. The meaning of life."

"Did you come back to GPSC after the war?"

"After the war I couldn't go back to math and science. I wanted more. I wanted a broader liberal arts education. I wanted to think through some of the issues that war presented to me. I left the farm, enrolled at the University of Oklahoma, and majored in "Letters," an interdisciplinary program in History, Literature, and Philosophy. I studied Classical Greek and took classes in Art History. It was a program that attempted to help students understand and appreciate the essence of western culture, the movements of the human mind from the Greeks to the present – the workings of Spirit, as Hegel might say.

"I enrolled in a philosophy course taught by Gustav Mueller, which turned out to be a life-changing experience for me. He had been hired by the university in 1930, a German-speaking, Swiss philosopher, a learned European intellectual with a Ph.D from the University of Bern. He was a specialist in Hegel but he wrote on everything: Plato, Marx, Freud, American Literature,

Homer, The Greek Tragedians, Shakespeare, Goethe, aesthetics, philosophy of education, philosophy of religion. He wrote plays that were performed by the OU School of Drama. He published six volumes of poetry. He wrote short stories. He translated Hegel. His learning was overwhelming."

As Professor Taylor was talking, I thought of Jim Burden and the young classics professor who assisted him in his mental awakening. It was a similar story, but Jim Burden decided he couldn't be a scholar.

I asked Professor Taylor: "So you didn't actually major in philosophy?"

"I majored in Mueller and took as many of his classes as I could. Professor Mueller became my mentor and friend and ideal. I completed my B.A., then an M.A. in Philosophy. My father became sick. I returned to help with the farm as his health worsened. He held on for three years before he died. If we were to keep the farm in the family I had to give up my goal of getting the Ph.D in philosophy. GPSC hired me to teach a course in the humanities, then another and another. The Dean kept me busy as an adjunct. Good fortune: I was hired to replace our full-time humanities professor, who retired. I was appointed an Assistant Professor, despite only having a masters degree. I introduced philosophy courses into the curriculum, and have, for many years, combined, rather oddly, two full-time jobs: college professor and farmer."

"Do you ever want to leave here?" I asked.

"There was a time when I considered giving up my position, getting a Ph.D somewhere, and living beyond the confines of northwest Oklahoma. But I'm fortunate to have this job, and I have learned to love the soil as much as I love the play of ideas and the grand march of philosophy. I travel in the summer, after the wheat harvest, in the down time between the cycles of working the fields. Next summer I'm going to Europe to visit Professor Mueller in Bern and to travel through southern Switzerland and northern Italy. Sils Maria. Montagnola. And at GPSC I get to teach some bright interested students – like Mrs. Wilson, your teacher. You're very lucky to have such a fine teacher of literature."

The epiphany took place on a sunny Sunday in September, the finest time of the year to play baseball on the Great Plains of northwest Oklahoma. At that time the weather decides to calm down and replace springtime torment with the placid and undisturbed warmth of Mother Earth's autumn friendliness. No huge winds that turn infield popups into challenging adventures, infielders into staggering drunks, and routine fly balls into extra base hits. No approaching thunderstorms that threaten to turn baseball dirt into muck. No surprise cold fronts from the north that cause shivering, under-dressed ballplayers to wish they had worn long sleeves and brought a jacket to the ballpark. Just a slight breeze from the south, a pleasing affection as you look into the sun, and the feeling that it's great to play ball on a day like this.

We met at the Conway High School baseball field for our weekly get-together, play and easy camaraderie – of course, Jake wasn't just my comrade and Josh was more like my brother. We had a routine: short toss to warm up, long toss to strengthen our arms, fly balls and grounders, batting practice, and we ended with Josh's bullpen session. Jake now had a catcher's mitt. For the session I stood behind Josh.

He had finally stopped growing and had filled out, the product of farm labor and Virginia's cooking. He was still lanky and raw-boned, with long arms and legs, slender not skinny, loose, flexible, smooth, effortless when he ran and threw a baseball. He was throwing harder; Jake wore a sponge in his mitt and sometimes clubbed one of Josh's pitches because he couldn't handle the speed and movement. Josh threw hard – harder than I had ever seen him throw.

In later years I thought a lot about the nature of an epiphany, the process (if there is one), the religious overtones, the background. I first thought of an epiphany as wholly subjective, a flash of insight, some realization that strikes in a moment – like the Buddhist experience of satori: sudden enlightenment. However, if an epiphany is an act of realization then something must be realized. If it is an act of seeing then something is seen. In some cases an epiphany is both subjective and objective – especially in cases of a purported appearance of a divine or superhuman being.

It must have been like that for Tom Greenwade when he first had the sudden understanding that Mickey Mantle was a superhuman baseball player – when the scout saw the Divine, "The Mick," in the seventeen year old. Mickey was an epiphany; Tom Greenwade had an epiphany – and now, here was Josh and my epiphany. My budding scouting experiences came together in a flash of understanding, informed by the big league pitchers I had seen that summer, and the eighteen year old recently-drafted "boy" I had seen in Tulsa, Jerry Reuss. My newly formed schema produced a comparison with Josh: similar statures, both threw left-handed, smooth delivery, similar arm angle, release point, leg kick, and stride. One was a high draft pick who would pitch in the major leagues for over twenty years, debuting at a mere twenty years old. The other had never played a game of organized baseball but looked like a better athlete who threw harder and whose pitches had better movement. A sudden striking realization. I saw the future. Josh is a prospect!

From that moment I was convinced that Josh had special talent, a tool that could make him transcendent in the world of baseball, an arm that could take him to the top. Perhaps I was mesmerized by the story of Mickey Mantle and the possibility of finding an extraordinary jewel in the most unlikely place. But this discovery would be even more astonishing because Josh had never played a game. How could he possibly be the pitching equivalent of The Mick? I told myself that it would be a mistake to confuse nature and culture. Why couldn't the blessed emerge in a place like Conway? If Commerce, why not Conway? The way the ball exploded out of Josh's hand had nothing to do with smallness of place and cultural scarcity. It was more like winning the lottery with a miniscule probability of success than taking advantage of opportunities provided in more populated settings.

My epiphany may have also been fired by a fantasy I had cultivated. Why couldn't a girl become a baseball scout? Coach Ross told me there had been one and only one female scout in the history of major league baseball. The Philadelphia Phillies hired Edith Houghton in 1946 and she lasted a few seasons. I saw myself in the stands, behind home plate, working for the Cardinals, seated among other scouts. I hear the whispers. "That's Lizzie Ware. She discovered Josh Kirchner. He hadn't even pitched in a real game and now he's probably a Hall of Famer."

I was exuberant. "Josh, you're a prospect!"

"What do you mean, I'm a prospect? Prospect for what?"

"You're a prospect for professional baseball. You have a plus fastball."

"What's a plus fastball?" Josh was perplexed.

"It's a fastball better than the major league average."

Jake was doubtful – probably envious. "How do you know that?"

"Because I can see it. Josh is better than a kid I saw this summer playing for the Tulsa Oilers, who was a second round draft choice for the Cardinals, their top pitching prospect. I think Josh has more potential than that pitcher, who is eighteen years old, just graduated from high school. Josh throws harder and his ball moves more."

"But I can't play real baseball. My father wouldn't let me."

"If he knew how good you are, how much potential you have, maybe he would reconsider. He might think your arm is a gift from God. We should ask him."

"Maybe."

"Would you throw for Coach Ross? Let's see what he thinks before we talk to your dad."

The next day I talked to Coach Ross. I told him I had discovered a pitching prospect with a plus fastball, right here in Conway High: Josh Kirchner. "I want you to take a look at him."

"But his family won't let him play sports. I've asked."

I explained to Coach Ross that Josh had been playing informally with Jake and me since he moved to Conway at the beginning of tenth grade, and that we had taught him a few things. "Just take a look, Coach. He's a natural. He throws hard, has good control, he's loose, good life on his fastball."

Later in the week, after baseball practice, Coach Ross asked our regular catcher to stay for a few minutes, to catch someone. I warmed up Josh in the outfield along the left field line, with Coach Ross by my side. "Stretch him out. I want to see him throw long." I motioned Josh to back up.

Coach Ross: "Really nice arm action. Nice carry. Good arm strength."

We walked to the bullpen. I stood with Coach Ross, behind Josh. Lawrence Dodd wore full catching gear. Jake stood right-handed at home plate to give Josh the feel of a real batter and strike zone. Lawrence gave the target: down the middle, knee high. Windup, right knee to the belt, hips closed, stride toward home plate, easy and smooth delivery, high ¾ release point – the ball exploded out of Josh's hand, crossed the plate with a little late movement, where Lawrence held his mitt. A loud crack filled the park as the ball smacked into its deep leather target.

Coach Ross whispered, barely audible. "Unbelievable."

After a few more pitches, Coach Ross instructed our catcher to change locations: outside, inside – up in the zone, down. Josh's control was impeccable.

"Josh, show me your grip."

He reached out his hand, with long, bony fingers across the big horseshoe seams, thumb and fourth finger on the bottom seams – a four-seamer, just as Jake and I had taught.

"Try this. It's called a two-seam grip. You might get more movement."

At first Josh had a more difficult time locating the two-seam fastball, because of the increased movement. The ball had better sinking action.

Coach Ross turned to me. "I don't think I've ever seen anything like this in a young pitcher. There are professional pitchers who would kill for that kind of late life. For Josh it seems natural with his loose wrist action, long fingers, and release point."

I asked, "Is it a plus fastball?"

"Yes, Lizzie, that's a plus fastball. Unbelievable. You found a prospect. It could turn into a plus-plus fastball when he fills out."

Coach Ross asked, "Do you throw a curveball or change-up?" The curve ball rolled rather than snapped. Josh just slowed his arm when he tried to throw a change.

"We can work on those pitches. And maybe tweak your mechanics a little, if you want to work with me."

"I would Coach. But my parents don't allow me to play sports. I don't think they would let me play for the team."

"Then we'll do it for fun. Maybe before next spring we can change their minds."

A few days later Coach asked Josh to help prepare the team for our game in the regional tournament, after we had won our district championship. We had to face a tough left hander in our game against Dover. "It wouldn't be a real game. Not super competitive. Just challenge our hitters to help them be better prepared when we face a hard thrower. Your father wouldn't object to that, would he? Throw batting practice; a couple of days later I'll have you throw a few innings in a simulated game."

Josh threw batting practice, harder than usual for us, but not nearly as hard as he could throw. He threw to nine batters in the simulated game. Seven strike outs, two weak grounders, and a broken bat for Jake when he was jammed by one of Josh's plus fastballs.

We didn't win the Class C Fall Baseball Championship, but we were sure that we could win in the spring, if we had Josh on the mound. And Coach Ross had an entire winter and early spring to polish a gem.

Another road trip,with my father and Coach Ross, to a town in the Texas panhandle, south of Amarillo, north of Lubbock: Plainview, population 15,000, West Texas desert-parched and teetotaler dry – which made the small city a fine Christian place in the eyes of Pastor Fred – and home of The Wayland Baptist Flying Queens, the best women's college basketball program in the whole damn country!

We could take one of two routes: down through the country to the interstate, west to Amarillo, south to Plainview; or we could mosey southwest through Woodward to Shattuck (again), find the Highway 60 diagonal through Pampa to Amarillo, and turn left. Both routes would involve five hours of flat nothing-ness. One would avoid the busy-ness of an interstate highway and force us to drive through more no-stoplight emptiness, the road lined with a few weather-beaten shacks. One route was faster, the other more deliberate. No contest. The pace of the driver's life (my dad's) had slowed to caution and predictability; the pace of divided highway traffic would be too much for his system – better to travel in two-lane repose. No rush. We left early. We were to meet someone from the admissions office at two o'clock for the campus tour; practice was at four.

Our trip was the product of contingency and enthusiasm. My number one community fan, Dale Parker, had known the Wayland Baptist coach, Harley Redin, when they served together in the Marines. And Coach Parker's enthusiasm was peaked by one of our games before the Christmas break. In our first conference matchup we played a good team in a close game. Afterwards I knew I had scored a lot of points but I didn't keep track. I was more pleased with my all-around game: passing, rebounding, some steals. I was stronger and quicker as a senior. I could jump higher and I was more athletic. Coach Ross never mentioned scoring in our post-game meetings. He talked about fundamentals, how hard we played, whether we had executed well, as a team, on offense and defense. The scorekeeper told me I had scored 52 points. I was used to putting up points because I had averaged over 25 points a game as a junior. This year we had few solid forwards, so I was supposed to shoot more often. I hadn't hogged the ball. I tried to play with my teammates but the game dictated more shots from our primary ball handler. My teammates deferred more often. I was in the zone and I kept shooting. I didn't want to leave the space in which I was lost in a momentary, relative perfection. The game was close, we won, and my play was excellent.

After the game Coach Parker congratulated me. He was excited and effusive. "Lizzie, you were terrific. We have to find a place for you to play next year."

He called his old friend at Wayland, Coach Redin, and a week later a date was set for my tryout, after the first of the year. We would drive to Plainview on a Friday, practice with the Flying Queens in late afternoon, stay with players in a dorm, and scrimmage with the team on Saturday morning. Back to Conway by Saturday evening, then report to Jean and Jake.

Wayland Baptist was one of the few colleges in the 1950s and 60s to have a women's basketball team. It was probably the first four-year college program to provide full scholarships to its female players and Wayland was certainly the only women's basketball team to fly to its away games. It was sponsored by the Hutcherson Flying Service of Plainview, Texas, owned by Claude and Wilda Hutcherson, who provided snazzy uniforms and flew the team thousands of miles in a season in company planes. It was dubbed the Hutcherson Flying Queens and competed mainly against industrial teams who were members of the Amateur Athletic Union (AAU). During the 1950s the Flying Queens had a 131 game consecutive winning streak and won four consecutive AAU National Championships. They traveled the country, played against the toughest veteran teams, flew in private planes, stayed in good hotels, and entertained fans in pre-game warmups with a Globetrotter routine, players in a circle, "Sweet Georgia Brown" blaring as they performed their tricks with the basketball. Each year the Queens attracted scores of young ladies to the campus for tryouts.

After my tryout we met in Coach Redin's office: Pastor Fred, Coach Ross, and a new recruit. "We have two scholarships open next year. They are full scholarships: tuition, room and board, books, and fees. I want to offer one of those scholarships to you, Miss Ware."

Smiles all around. I could see the future and it was good.

"If you accept the scholarship and attend Wayland Baptist and play for the Flying Queens you will be required to sign the Wayland Pledge: to refrain from cursing, smoking, drinking, and pre-marital sex, and you will be required to attend mandatory chapel and church services each week. I want to make it clear that this is a Baptist institution."

Pastor Fred interjected, "That wouldn't be a problem. That's excellent, isn't it Lizzie?"

"No problem," I said. "That's great." In fact, I wondered about the Baptist part of Wayland Baptist University. But after spending an evening with a few of the Flying Queens, I realized the pledge wouldn't be an issue. No doubt there were a few devout Baptists on the team and one or two tepid Methodists. As far as I could tell some of the girls' devotion to the pledge was selective and situational. It depended on the audience.

Paster Fred had no idea that some of my philosophical conversations with Professor Enos Taylor were leading me in the direction of my philosophy instructor's Buddhist - flavored agnosticism and religious pluralism - and away from the preacher's exclusivist claims about the sole path to Truth, salvation, and an eternal human destiny in heaven. Despite years of listening to hundreds of my father's sermons - and interminable household religious instruction - I was becoming genuinely puzzled about the existence of God and the source of religious truth. But playing for the Flying Queens need not keep me from thinking, as my philosophy mentor would insist.

Coach Redin continued his sales pitch. "There's another thing that might interest you. Coach Ross tells me that you may be a better baseball and softball player than a basketball player."

"I don't know about that," I said.

"There's a girls' baseball team up in Amarillo. They travel all over Texas and the region and play semi-pro teams, both men's and women's teams. I know the coach and could get you a tryout. If you make the team you would stay with a host family during the summer and be provided with a job that allows the flexibility to travel. If you're as good as Coach Ross says, you'd have a good chance to make the team."

I wasn't quite sure how these prospects would affect my relationship with Jake, but I knew I wanted to keep playing basketball – with the Flying Queens! – and the possibility that I could play baseball left me thunderstruck. I had a new plan. I would play for the Flying Queens for a year or two, spend summers away from Conway and my family's Christian rigidity, and I could re-assess my future after that. I wanted to go to OU, major in Letters, study literature and philosophy. I could use some of the money I inherited from Harry Berens to pay tuition – but first I wanted to be a college athlete and I wanted to play baseball.

Coach Redin stood up, shook hands all around, and closed the pitch. "We want you to be a Flying Queen. I'll send papers for you to sign later in the spring. We hope to see you on campus next fall."

I had my eighteenth birthday party in Harding, Kansas, just across the state line, past the "Welcome to Kansas" sign, past the salvage yard and the railroad tracks, into the depths of sin, twelve miles north of Alma. There wasn't much to Harding: a general store, bank, diner, and elementary school. One stoplight, which wasn't a fully functioning multi-colored device. It just flashed red twenty-four hours a day, no more efficient and certainly more costly than putting stop signs at the main intersection. The tiny town was a few blocks square, except when heading west from the stoplight, which put a tourist in open country immediately.

I had been through Harding only once, with Jake and friends headed west, nothing for twenty miles until we reached a canyon containing the opening to the Bat Caves, filled with mountains of guano, bat poop, and endless spooky black passages for teenage spelunkers.

Despite Harding's nondescript appearance, it was always spring break on Friday and Saturday nights, because the legal drinking age in Kansas was eighteen years old and the proprietors of the two dingy bars in town were uninterested in the minor details of enforcing the liquor laws, for example, verifying that a customer was actually eighteen years old. If a young local appeared to be in the neighborhood of the late teen years, give or take a couple or three years, no problem – no ID. Put your money on the bar. The loose atmosphere kept traffic flowing from the south, where a person had to be twenty-one to buy beer in Oklahoma. A mythology about one of the bars was passed down to prospective underage lawbreakers. "How old do you have to be to buy a draw at Ginders? Old enough to reach up and put your quarter on the bar!"

I heard the stories and knew my boyfriend was an experienced Kansas criminal. However, I was naturally cautious. No underage boozing for me. After all, I was a preacher's kid. Jake convinced me that the perfect spot to celebrate my eighteenth birthday was at Ginders: dark, symbolizing my fall into adulthood, but festive and communal. Jake was in charge of the invitations to some of my classmates, including Marcia, who was an illegal. We sat around a big round table in the corner, played pool badly, and laughed our way from normal consciousness, to being buzzed, to something more. My friends thought it was hilarious that the preacher's kid was sipping from a glass of Coors. Some of them had heard Pastor Fred preach about the sins of alcohol. I didn't much like the taste of beer, but I liked my friends and I endorsed teenage rebellion and the attempt to play adult.

Jake's sinfulness wasn't so very different from my other male classmates' transgressions. The rites of passage were similar. A cigar or cigarette behind the barn. The first dizzying can of beer. Rum in a Sonic coke. Slow dancing at the sock hop in the school gymnasium. A well-chosen "shit" or "hell" or "goddamn" in speech to friends. The signs of approaching adulthood were the ones that Wayland Baptist University was keen to extinguish in its college students – unsuccessfully. Jake wasn't wild, but he had a small-town wild streak of which I approved. He introduced me to Conway, farming, and my own first steps of walking on the wild side, according to the conventions of teenage life in the 1960s in northwest Oklahoma – an unsurprising irony associated with conventions and conventional revolt.

In other respects Jake was a typical farm boy. He didn't understand my interest in literature and philosophy. We didn't talk about Mrs. Wilson's English class, about *King Lear* or Wordsworth or Dickens. He found the romantic's love of nature ridiculous. His politics consisted of flag-waving, overt comments about loving his country, and claims about the need to stop the spread of Communism in Southeast Asia. He would have joined the Army after high school graduation if not for his desire to play college baseball and become a teacher and a coach.

Jake was wary of a more substantive counter-cultural rebellion. On Christmas vacation we were invited to Marcia's house to meet her older brother Al, visiting from Oklahoma City, where he lived, played music, and gambled. Small, with longer hair than was acceptable in Conway, liberal politics, and beat sensibilities. Years earlier he had taken piano lessons with Vera Tucker, advanced to instruction from a member of the music faculty at GPSC, and majored in music at the college for two years, until he joined the Air Force. Stationed in Germany, discovered the jazz scene in Europe, and came back to Oklahoma with changed musical tastes and no ambition to settle into a middle class style of life – much to the dismay of Dr. and Mrs. Little.

Despite looking scruffy, Al had an aura of experience and sophistication. Marcia asked him to play for us. "Play something by Bill Evans." He sat at the Little's piano, put his head down and closed his eyes, as if he was entering a trance – communicating with a jazz piano genius.

He first played "Waltz for Debby," which started slowly, turned up the volume, and began to swing. I could imagine the other members of a trio knitting the lines together as one. Al ended and smiled; we clapped. Marcia said, "One more."

He played "Re: Person I Knew," which became my favorite Bill Evans' tune. I entered into Al's trance – Bill Evans' trance. The emotional tone was quite different from the swinging waltz we had just heard. It was impressionistic, introspective, calm but tempestuous. The rounded phrases of the right hand captured, for me, the mood of a day, the rhythm of experience: unrest, ceaseless motion, movement into the future without a clear goal. The music didn't quite know where it was going; as the right hand wandered, the left hand stayed home to still the striving – a sense of circularity with a light touch. There was nostalgia and quiet optimism in the searching interaction between Al's right hand, overworked and probing, and his left hand, which remained grounded.

I was moved, full of something, but I knew not what. I didn't know how to articulate the notion that music sounds as feelings feel: experience has a form that can be represented by sound, and music can make one feel the mystery of being enmeshed in the flow of time. Later, when I listened to Bill Evans play the same pieces that Al played for us that night, I was astonished by Al's virtuosity. He had transcribed Evans' compositions, note for note, and transformed improvisation into devotional imitation. The music was a different kind of Altar Call, and I would, from that day forward, be a member of the Church of Bill Evans.

My boyfriend Jake was completely unmoved, like an atheist who is tone-deaf to his partner's life-altering religious experience. And when Al deftly rolled a joint, lit up, deeply inhaled and passed it around, I knew I had to try, because I had entered another world. Jake demurred, as I surrendered to an embarrassing fit of coughing. And he seemed to be a little jealous when I talked to Al about the book he was reading: *On the Road*, by Jack Kerouac. I told him I loved Whitman. He urged me to read *Howl*, by Kerouac's poetic friend, a contemporary Walt Whitman: Allen

Ginsberg. Al was another teacher, unexpected in Conway. Ginsberg taught Kerouac the aesthetic power of spontaneous prose, Al said. "You have to read Kerouac." For a few days after I met Al, I was "on the road."

Despite our differences, Jake and I shared commonalities that were much more important. We were recognized as a pair; we were "going steady". Of course we were different, but I seemed to be different from all of my high school friends. It didn't matter. I loved to be with Jake. He was so much fun and full of life. He made me laugh and called me back to earth when my thoughts took flight from the fields we inhabited. And we regularly went parking, another kind of fun and excitement I shared with Jake.

After my trip to Plainview, Texas, we talked more about our future, since it was apparently going to involve some prolonged absences from one another. In my mind, we would sustain our relationship through college, then seal the deal. The OU part of my plan began to fade. I would major in English, become certified to teach, and we would live happily ever after, making athletic babies, sustaining the Tucker's farm somehow, and rooting for the St. Louis Cardinals.

The events of our last semester at Conway High School would change all of that.

Basketball season ended with a whimper, not a bang, since we didn't get to the state tournament, nor did the boys team. The weather warmed, the southern breezes returned, and our thoughts turned to baseball.

Josh had been working with Coach Ross through the winter months, outside when the weather allowed, in the gymnasium when the north winds were howling and the water froze in animal troughs. They threw at least twice a week, worked on Josh's mechanics and secondary pitches – curve ball and changeup – and added a cut fastball (a cutter) to his repertoire. I watched as Coach Ross refined the tools, sharpened and polished and honed. Josh was a model student, open to being coached and so naturally gifted that the path from instruction to performance was flawless.

The master shows the student a new grip: slightly off-center, more pressure on the middle finger, the ball held loosely and lovingly in long, slender fingers. Perhaps a slight turn of the wrist and thrown like a fastball – but not far from home plate the ball takes a nasty little six-inch right turn, into the hands of a right-handed batter. Josh would now have an added weapon: a cut fastball.

Josh often carried a baseball with him as he walked the halls of Conway High School, middle finger at twelve o'clock on a big seam, thumb at six o'clock on another seam. He practices a curve ball release, almost like snapping his fingers, to impart maximal spin on the pitch – heavy rotation as the ball appears to be in the strike zone but ends in the dirt behind home plate.

We knew where the pitching coach's expert instruction was heading. For Josh to be able to pursue his craft, John would have to give permission to his son to play baseball for Conway High. A meeting with Josh's parents was scheduled. Coach Ross asked me to attend since the Kirchners were my close friends, and perhaps I could be persuasive. We met after school, the day before baseball practice was to begin: John, Virginia, Josh, Coach Ross, and Lizzie, in their country kitchen. (Ruth was listening in the next room.)

Coach Ross got to the point. He explained that he had been working with Josh at school. Your son has extraordinary gifts, he said. He's the best high school pitching prospect I've ever seen, and I've been playing, coaching, and scouting for many, many years. Yes, if you let Josh play it would be great for our team. I think we could win the state championship. But Josh's future is bright well beyond what happens this spring. I think he has a future in professional baseball. Talent like Josh's doesn't come around often. I can think, he said, of only one other time that I've been so struck by the natural gifts of a baseball player. That player was also from a small town in Oklahoma and he became one of the greats of all time.

My strategy was to play in John's ballpark, since he had a home field advantage. I said that Josh's natural talent was a gift from God, and it would be a shame not to allow him to use and express the blessings bestowed by God. Sports don't necessarily harm a person's character. Players can respect their opponents and be thankful for the abilities they have been given and the opportunities to use their God-given talents (although by this time I was more inclined to say that we should be grateful for being lucky in the natural lottery).

John was nice; Virginia kept silent. They didn't question why the coach had been instructing their son without telling the parents. If Josh was having fun learning new things, that's fine. But John had not changed his mind. He said his highest goal as a parent was to teach his children to be like Christ, to love one another as Christ loves us. He reiterated his view that competition taught the wrong things to young people. When one team wins, the other loses. By attempting to win you want your opponents to lose; the goals of opponents in competitive activities are mutually exclusive and athletic desires are selfish. No. He said he would not allow Josh to play baseball.

Josh: "Dad, I'd really like to play. I promise I'll treat my opponents with respect."

"But son, you want them to lose. You want to defeat them and embarrass them. I can't allow it. We must love our neighbors, as Christ teaches us. Sports are for others, but not for us."

"Yes, Father." In my mind I connected this scene with the senseless death of Sarah. It was hard for me to understand how parents who loved their children so much could allow their religion to cause distress and disappointment. Josh was crushed. John and Virginia couldn't see the future as Coach Ross and I could. Or did they see a future in which baseball success wasn't very important?

The meeting ended cordially. Coach Ross shook hands with both parents. "Would you let Josh practice with us sometimes, just to help the team? Throw batting practice? No real competition – if Josh wants to help us?"

"I'd like that dad."

John looked at Virginia and she seemed to offer a slight nod. "I suppose a little practice to help the team would be all right."

We ended the meeting with a new batting practice pitcher, but I sensed that Coach Ross hadn't given up. The arrangement would be a way for the pupil to keep his arm in shape while the artist attempted to liberate the image from a block of unformed shiny marble.

In March, 1968, LBJ announced that he would not seek re-election. The Vietnam War was seething. The civil disorders of the previous long hot summer were lingering in the public mind. Martin Luther King, Jr., was shot and killed in Memphis in early April, sending cities into flaming seats of division. The next President of the United States, Robert Kennedy, was shot in a Los Angeles hotel after winning the California primary. He died the next day. The nation was blowing up – and in Conway, Oklahoma, the impossible had happened. The world was falling apart and my tidy little part of it mirrored the whole.

The chances of it happening were slight: one late afternoon at the Tucker's farm when Vera was gone and two kids lost control. We were young and foolish. There was no guilt because we were in love, pledged, almost, to be married some day – but I worried. What if? I missed a monthly and denial set in. These things happened to other girls with bad reputations, not girls who were smart, athletic, well-liked, made good grades, and…it couldn't happen to a preacher's kid. I thought: if I ignore the possibility it will go away. I didn't feel any different, but I felt stupid.

The second miss changed things: queasy mornings and tenderness where there had been none before. I told no one. I was frightened and depressed. Jake could tell something was wrong. I kept up a good face in front of my parents but a sense of impending ruin was becoming impossible to deny or ignore. I couldn't stop nature from running its course. I wanted time to stop or go backward. I did not see how a future with this new reality would be possible.

At first the feeling wasn't misery; it was disbelief. It was utter disbelief, like trying to believe a contradiction. I wanted to live in a world in which overwhelming evidence for something was the sign of its opposite. I'm just a little off; I probably have some kind of bug, I thought. I'm sure it will go away; maybe it's just stress about the future. After my first miss I did 100 sit-ups a day and worked out harder, hoping it would help me get my period. Something is wrong in there; it can't be a baby. After the second miss I knew I had to see a doctor.

I couldn't go to our family physician, Marcia's dad, Dr. Little. I didn't want him to know. I made an appointment with a doctor in Alma, after school. My parents thought I was going to shop. The test was performed and my false hopes were squashed. The test came back positive. I started to bawl uncontrollably. I sobbed and sobbed, the tears ran down my cheeks, my chest heaved, and the world became more dim behind a curtain of despair. A future that had been as bright as Mickey's as he left high school now faded into hopelessness. There could be no future now.

I calmed down and wiped my eyes. I wanted the doctor to hug me but that would have been unprofessional. He spoke with compassion; he knew I needed help.

"Have you told your parents?"

"No."

"Have you told your boyfriend?"

"No."

"Lizzie, this doesn't have to be the end of the world. Other girls have gone through this. Let the people who love you help. You're not alone."

At that moment I thought more about what it would be like to tell Pastor Fred than how Jake would react.

"Did you come alone?"

"Yes."

"Do you think you can drive home by yourself?"

"Yes."

I took a deep breath and walked out of the doctor's office, past the receptionist, through the waiting room. I felt as if everyone was staring at me because my face was flushed and I was unsteady. I stepped outside into an April day, a baseball day, that should have heightened my senses with its brilliant sunshine and calming breezes. But today it did nothing to pierce the veil of my despair. I was cloaked in insensibility. I have no memory of the drive back to Conway.

I called Jake. "We have to talk."

"What about?"

"It's something serious. I'll drive out after supper."

Jake was in the yard when I turned up the driveway. He met me with a hug and a peck on the mouth.

"Let's go inside. My mom went to Conway for choir practice."

We sat down on Vera's ugly flowered couch.

"Jake, I have something to tell you." I was silent for a few moments. I couldn't get the words out of my mouth. My lips quivered. My eyes watered. "I'm pregnant."

"You're pregnant." He said the word back to me as if he was trying to decipher some strange word in a foreign language.

"Yes, I'm pregnant."

"Are you sure?"

"Yes, Jake, I went to Alma this afternoon for a pregnancy test and it came back positive."

"But how is that possible?"

"You know how it's possible."

"But it was only one time."

"That's all it takes, Jake."

"Shit. What are we going to do?"

"I don't know."

"Have you told anyone?"

"No, I haven't told anyone. I have to tell my parents." I was trying to interpret the look on his face. Shock? Disbelief? Disappointment? Kind of like striking out with the bases loaded in the bottom of the ninth? I wondered if his life was passing before his mind in a jumbled moment, as mine had when I first found out.

"I'm scared Jake. I'm so scared." He reached out and took me into his big farm arms and held me as I started to sob again.

"Lizzie, we can make this work. I guess we could get married. Couldn't we?"

A new complication had arisen. He had been offered a small scholarship to play baseball at Oklahoma State. The offer was books – nothing more. Vera had that proud-parent radiance and announced to everyone in the community that Jake was going to OSU on a baseball scholarship – which was technically correct. She thought Jake's baseball career was ready to take off. Instead of going to GPSC and playing small college baseball he would play big-time baseball and have a chance to "go pro," as she said. How was a baby going to figure into Vera's plans for Jake?

We talked until we heard Vera's car come up the driveway. She greeted us cheerfully as I stood up to leave.

"How are you kids doing?" She always called us kids. For Vera, we were just kids.

Jake said, "We'll talk tomorrow."

The next day he reported his conversation with Vera.

"Mom, I have something to tell you. Lizzie is pregnant."

"Pregnant! Are you sure?"

"She had the test and it came back positive."

"Goddammit, Jake! What were you thinking?"

"I wasn't thinking, Mom."

"No, you weren't thinking. Don't you know what a goddamned rubber is?"

I blushed when Jake told me that she called a condom a "rubber."

"Mom! It wasn't planned. It just happened."

"It just happened. Is that all you have to say? When is she due?"

"In November."

"Jesus Christ, Jake. I can't believe this." Vera was a profane Christian.

"Mom, we can make this work. Maybe we could get married."

"Married? You're too young to get married, Jake. You can't get married. You're going to OSU and play baseball. You don't know how to take care of a baby. Where would you live? How would you support a wife and baby?"

"You could help us. Then some day I could pay you back."

"No, Jake, you're not getting married. That would be foolish. We'll have to talk with Pastor Fred and Jean. Has Lizzie told her parents?"

"No, but she's going to tell them when she gets back to Conway."

When I returned to Conway I thought I may as well get it over with. Entering the parsonage was like walking toward a land mine waiting to explode. My mom and dad were sitting in the living room watching television.

"Hi. Could we turn off the TV? I have something to tell you." My voice was shaking. They could tell that my news couldn't wait until the next commercial break or when Bonanza was over.

"I'm sorry. I'm so sorry. I'm pregnant."

They looked at me, uncomprehending for a few moments, until my simple declaration reached into them like other pieces of horrible news we get in life: Harry died; Sarah didn't make it; Lizzie is pregnant. They had constructed me as an ideal – in a moment, I had destroyed their notion of me.

My mom started sobbing, as I did. She reached out for me, took me into her arms, and rocked me side to side like a little girl. She spoke softly.

"Oh Lizzie, Lizzie, Lizzie. What have you done?" Her embrace was an expression of both love and remorse. I knew forgiveness was there for the asking.

I said it again. "I'm so sorry, Mom. We didn't mean to. It just happened. We love each other, but I know it wasn't right."

My dad got up from the couch and started pacing, as he did when he delivered a sermon. When he was agitated he couldn't sit still. His face was red and his jaw was tight. I waited for the explosion. I didn't have to wait very long.

"Young lady, you have sinned against the Lord. You have shamed and dishonored us. You have let Satan into your life. Have you prayed for forgiveness?"

I wanted him to take me into his arms and tell me he loved me and that everything would be alright. I wanted my baseball-loving daddy, not Pastor Fred. But he was Old School, in baseball and religion. Don't rub it. When you get knocked down, get back up. Be tough. Don't whine. Don't show your emotions. If you have sinned, get on your knees.

"I'm sorry, Father. I hope you'll forgive me."

"It's not my forgiveness that you need. Have you asked the Lord for forgiveness?"

No, I hadn't, but I didn't tell Pastor Fred. I did what I did, it was stupid, and I was sorry. But if the Lord was there, I was sure he still loved me, despite my transgressions. I couldn't say the words my father wanted me to say. We stared at each other. I thought it was time to leave the room. As I walked to my bedroom, I heard my mother.

"We love you, Lizzie."

Later, after I had gone to bed, I tried to calm down and recuperate in the darkness. I couldn't sleep; my monkey-mind did what it wanted. I heard the door open, a slender light appeared from the hallway, and I could see my father looking into my bedroom, to see whether my lamp was still on, to see whether I was still awake. The light didn't reach my face. I could see him but he couldn't see me. He looked for a few precious seconds into the darkness, then closed the door. As it was closing, I called out to him.

"Daddy, I'm still awake."

The door opened a second time. He stood by my bed, leaned down, and kissed my cheek.

"I just wanted to kiss you good night, Lizzie, like I used to."

"Thanks."

"Remember how I used to tell you baseball stories at bedtime when you were little?"

"Yes. I loved the one about Enos Slaughter."

"You'll get through this Lizzie, with the help of the Lord. Be sure to say your prayers. Let's play catch tomorrow."

"Okay, Dad, let's play catch tomorrow."

In the next few days I could tell that my father was at war with himself. He never mentioned my "trouble" and he acted as if nothing had happened. He was civil but cool, distant and disturbed. For Pastor Fred, being a preacher was more than a role; it was his identity. The religion that shaped that identity seemed to squelch the natural human sentiments that I so badly needed. I needed love, not judgment.

I felt sorry for him because I knew he was in pain and I had caused it. And it was strange that I felt more sorry for him than I did for myself. I thought that love could assuage the pain, or shame, or dishonor – whatever he was feeling. But for Pastor Fred these were religiously imbued emotions crowding out the father-daughter ones. His Father was more important than being my father.

I loved my father. He was a good man in many respects. He fed hungry strangers and made loans to the down-and-out when the car broke down or there was a delinquent utility bill. There was love in his heart, yet it felt abstract and unreal, filtered through religious concepts, directed toward "children of God" rather than particular, unreplaceable individuals. His love seemed more like Christian obligation than compassionate fellow feeling. I knew my father loved me, but Pastor Fred got in the way. The man who taught me to love and play baseball, and to keep score, and to root for the Cardinals, was dominated by the other person, subsumed by other-worldly concerns and the veneer of dogma. At the moment I needed a father, not the Preacher. There was a break that would never be healed. He walked away, never to return.

There was a meeting. Aggrieved parents and youthful sinners; adults, and the children they controlled. Jake and I had talked and talked, but our conversations were more therapeutic than practical. Vera walked into the parsonage, shook hands with my mother and Pastor Fred. We sat down. My father took a chair across the room, a detached spectator.

Vera spoke first.

"What are we going to do with these kids?"

The kids sat silent.

"I don't think marriage is a good idea, at their age."

My mom answered: "We don't think they should get married. We don't think they are ready to make a family and care for a baby."

"Jake is going to OSU. I don't see how it would work if they were married. How would they support themselves?"

No one asked us what we wanted. No one spoke to us. We didn't even hold hands. It would have reminded them of our illegitimate intimacy.

"We have worked out a plan," my mother said. She had run it by me, more as a matter of informing me about what would occur than asking for my approval.

"My sister Joan and her husband Virgil have moved to Oklahoma City for his work. They have offered to take Lizzie in until the baby is born. They have a small one bedroom garage apartment that will be perfect for her."

Aunt Joan and Uncle Virgil were nice people. That part of the plan sounded fine.

"We have contacted a Methodist social services agency to handle the adoption."

My future after that was uncertain. My parents would manufacture a plausible cover story – odd for the preacher to choose dishonesty over public embarrassment. It was obvious that my father didn't want me to return to Conway after the baby was born. He rarely talked to me now. I couldn't tell what my mother thought about giving the baby up for adoption. I think she was overwhelmed and subservient to the wishes of Pastor Fred.

Vera was relieved. "That sounds like a very good plan."

I wondered whether I might be able to stay longer with Aunt Joan and Uncle Virgil, past November, maybe go to Junior College in the City. There would be no basketball in my future.

My father rose and walked across the room.

"Could we join hands and pray?" I stood between my mother and Jake as Pastor Fred called on the Lord to forgive us of our sins and guide us in the future.

"Amen."

After the meeting I called Coach Redin at Wayland Baptist and told him I had decided that I wouldn't be playing for the Flying Queens. My plans had changed. He wished me good luck.

There was another person whose prospects in life were at issue that summer, my pregnant summer. I needed something to take my mind away from my own gloomy future, so I invested my hopes in the prospect I had discovered and a tool that would project him into glory. His late life would give me some compensation for my muddled later life.

It's late June, after the Major League draft. I remember vividly this piece of my last summer in Conway. A final baseball road trip with Coach Ross, this time without my father, who still wasn't saying much to me. It's a trip to the Oklahoma State University baseball field. It's cloaked in a bit of subterfuge, a little deceptiveness falling short of a big lie. Coach Ross and I worked out the plan together – baseball was helping me to forget. We're headed to a Saturday morning New York Yankees tryout camp, to be run by the current area scout, Lincoln Barr, an aging Tom Greenwade (who scouted only part-time now), and a bird-dog, Coach Ross. We're supposed to be taking Jake to his first tryout camp, organized for the purpose of evaluating players who may have been missed in the draft or younger players the scouts hoped to follow in the next year. We are really there to let them see Josh throw. Mr. Greenwade made the trip because of Coach Ross's sparkling evaluation. "You have to see this boy throw. You won't believe this is a kid who has never played in an organized game. It'll be worth the drive."

Coach Ross asked Josh to come along, to see Jake try out. "Bring your glove and spikes. Maybe you can help him warm up. It'll be a fun trip. Lizzie's going also. You know how she loves baseball."

We arrived early to sign up, along with fifty other players. Everyone received a number, attached to his jersey. Jake was now "Number 12," not Jake. Josh didn't sign up or receive a number, but the scouts knew who he was and why he was there.

Coach Ross had explained the structure of the tryout, which would be slow and unexciting. Remember: scouts are there to evaluate tools. The morning session consisted of timing each player twice in the sixty yard dash, a period of warmup for arms, then an evaluation of arm strength: three throws from deep shortstop or from rightfield to third base. As the position players threw, pitchers were allotted throws in the bullpen. A position player could also go to the bullpen and try out as a pitcher. Then each position player took six swings from a batting practice pitcher, who had been recruited independently. At the end of the morning session the head scout gathered the players in a group, thanked them for coming, encouraged them to keep working hard to improve their skills, and called out the numbers of the players who were invited to return after lunch for the afternoon session: a game with live pitching and hitting.

Each player was timed in the sixty – even pitchers – because it was one way to evaluate a player's athleticism. One scout was the starter, the other two were stationed at the finish line, timing a separate player. Coach Ross, the starter, called out to Josh, who was hanging toward the back of the group of players: "Jump in there with Jake." Mutt and Jeff. Jake had barely reached 5'9" by his senior year; Josh was almost 6'4". Short and choppy versus long and lean and smooth. Jake ran a 7.0, then a 6.9. Josh ran a 6.5, then 6.4, the fastest time in camp. After Josh ran his 6.5 Lincoln Barr looked at his stopwatch, did a double-take, held up his watch to Tom Greenwade, and said something.

After players loosened their arms, Coach Ross again called out to Josh: "Go out and throw from right field." I was sitting directly behind home plate. After Josh threw three missiles from right to third base, on a line, perfect one-hop throws – as we had taught him – I heard the area scout say to Coach Ross, who was hitting fungoes, "That's a plus arm."

"Wait till you see him throw off the mound."

Josh was the last pitcher to throw in the bullpen, before batting practice. The players were milling around the third base dugout. I moved down toward the bullpen. All three scouts were watching Josh throw. First, a few fastballs. "Josh, throw the cutter." The area scout smiled. "Now the curve." They looked at each other. No one said anything; they turned and walked back to home plate for batting practice.

I thought Jake did well at the tryout. He showed he was a solid ballplayer who might have a chance to contribute to a good college baseball team: adequate, not great speed, good hands, quick feet, not big power but solid gap-to-gap potential for extra base hits, didn't strike out much, and hit a lot of balls on the barrel of the bat. A good player, but he was not a prospect, despite Vera's expert evaluation of his abilities.

Jake's number wasn't called for the afternoon game, and since Josh didn't have a number, I thought we were ready to drive home at the end of the morning session. I saw the area scout walk over to Josh and briefly talk to him. Josh grinned and met Jake and me.

"What did he say?" I asked.

"He wants to see me throw in the afternoon game."

Jake slumped his shoulders and frowned. He asked, "Are you going to do it? Are you worried about what your father would say?"

"I guess I'll stay for the afternoon game, if it's alright with Coach Ross."

Josh was the first pitcher to throw in the afternoon game: two innings. (Other pitchers threw only one inning.) Six batters up – six batters down. Five strike outs and a weak grounder. A dominating, moving fastball, a few cutters on the inside part of the plate, and sharp, downward-breaking curves with heavy rotation. Overpowering stuff. Precise location – nothing in the middle of the plate. Surprising poise – no sign of nervousness, since he didn't understand what was going on. He was showcasing his raw but tutored talents – thanks to Coach Ross – for scouts who could sign him to a professional contract. He was oblivious. For Josh it was like throwing off the mound at Conway High in a simulated game.

There was a buzz among the players as Josh blew away the hitters, a man-child among boys. I saw Lincoln Barr and Tom Greenwade talk after Josh left the mound.

After the tryout ended Coach Ross invited me on to the field to meet the scouts. "Lizzie, I would like you to meet Tom Greenwade, the scout who discovered and signed Mickey Mantle, and Lincoln Barr, who covers Oklahoma, Kansas, and Missouri for the Yankees." They were cordial and welcoming. "And gentlemen, I want you to meet Lizzie Ware. She discovered Josh Kirchner and convinced me I should watch him throw."

Tom Greenwade spoke. "Remarkable, Miss Ware, just remarkable. I've been scouting for over thirty years and Josh Kirchner may be the best pitching prospect I've ever seen. And he's never pitched in a real game! Amazing. How did you find him? How did you decide he's a prospect?"

I told him my story: high school informal play, scouting instruction, a summer of evaluating the tools of major league players and the night in Tulsa I watched Jerry Reuss pitch.

Lincoln Barr: "Josh has fluid, natural arm strength, already a plus fastball – but it's the movement that sets his fastball apart. It's all about late life. Best late life I've ever seen! He's got a future. We could put him in a Double A uniform tomorrow and he'd be at the top of the rotation. He just needs innings. I think he could pitch in the big leagues in a couple of years. After that, the sky's the limit."

Tom Greenwade added, "Miss Ware, I had the same feeling watching Josh throw as I had when I first saw Mickey play. I could see the potential for greatness, later in his baseball life. You may have discovered a 'Great One.'"

Coach Ross had explained what scouts call a "signability problem." "We'll have to convince Josh's father to let him play, won't we?" He looked at me. "Lizzie, some day you may be famous."

A week later we had another meeting at the Kirchners' house. I was allowed to attend because I was now officially a bird-dog working for a bird-dog. Lincoln Barr was there representing the Yankees; Coach Ross and I were there as friends of Josh and to provide some context. The Yankees offered a $10,000 signing bonus and $500 a month in salary. They had a plan for developing Josh, until the end of summer, at a minor league training site, maybe a few innings in real games before the end of the season. He would report to spring training next March and be assigned to a team, probably in Class A. Mr. Barr said he was optimistic that Josh had the opportunity to advance quickly in the Yankee's minor league system.

Josh wanted to sign and the Kirchners needed the money. John again explained that what was most important was to teach his children to live as Jesus Christ had lived, and that competitive sport was a danger for Josh's character. The meeting ended in uncertainty rather than an outright rejection of the Yankees' offer. John said that he and Virginia – and Josh? – would pray for guidance and help from God. I thought about Sarah's illness, the Kirchners' prayers, and how my life had been inundated with Christianity since my first childhood prayers back in Missouri.

Another vivid memory from that memorable summer, a time of harvest and optimism in the community. It was to be my last harvest; once again I was a spectator rather than a liturgical participant. Jake invited me to the service.

"We're going to start cutting tomorrow. I'm going to drive the combine this year. My mom is driving the truck. Why don't you come out to the field tomorrow afternoon – the south place?"

I pull up to the field and see his machine far across the vast sunny plain. Vera waves but doesn't get out of the truck. Jake makes his round and stops about 100 feet into the field. He waves from the platform of the combine and steps down as I walk through the yellow stubble. He has a big boyish grin on his dirty face as he removes his goggles: large white circles around his sunburnt face, jeans with grease stains, reddish brown arms emerging from a dusty T-shirt, a grimy green John Deere hat. He's lined with the dust of the crop he's harvesting – and he looks like he had just hit a homerun. He's wearing dirt, as he does on a baseball field.

"I'd hug you but I'm too dirty."

"That's okay. I don't mind the dirt." We embrace; he smells earthy.

"Lizzie, you look great."

"No I don't, Jake. I feel fat. You look like a reverse racoon." He grins.

"Do you want to make a round with me?"

"Sure."

We climb up onto the machine and now we're moving, on top of the world. Up there on the platform I look down on the rotating reel, like the wheel on a steamboat, round and round, pushing the shoots of wheat into the header where the revolving auger sends the raw material into the guts of the machine to be threshed, separated, the grain finding its way to the bin behind us. Up there on the platform of the combine, high above the moving, rolling sea of gold, maneuvering that monstrous machine like a maestro in command of his orchestra, Jake is where he is meant to be – not because of some transcendent Plan, but because the ingredients that the world contributed to his young life combined with the dispositions of his inner being to place him just so, without any yearning to be elsewhere. For Jake, the farm is like the love he has for his Wilson A2000 fielder's glove, flawlessly shaped and oiled and cared for – hand and leather one with each other, an impeccable fit. He is at home in a world that is friendly and welcoming. There is for him a satisfying unity between self and world.

Life for Jake would be good; I was certain of that. But I was unsure whether I would ever be a part of it, despite what we had talked about. In the near future I would leave the comfort of Conway. I had been tutored by another fine teacher for a life rooted in the fields, but I was unsure whether I would be back for the next harvest.

My mother and I left Conway in July, almost four years to the day after we had arrived to make an insulated life in a small town in northwest Oklahoma. Pastor Fred was too busy pastoring to drive with us or to show his loving support for me. He was increasingly agitated when he looked at me. By midsummer I wore over-sized T-shirts to hide my sin but my wardrobe reminded him of my downfall. I was returning to the big city from which we had fled to protect my innocence. Conway was supposed to be a benign shelter from the more insidious influences of modern life: sex, drugs, rock and roll, and integration. I left with a profound sense of loss, but also a trace of hope.

I had lost my septuagenarian friend who bequeathed to me a tattered Whitman and money that would be invaluable in an uncertain future. I lost someone, a little sister, whose death was senseless. I lost my faith and my father. I ruined my chance to play college basketball for the Flying Queens – and maybe even play semi-pro baseball. I lost my home in Conway and I sensed that I was losing my best friend who became someone I loved. Our relationship was fraying. He may not have been mature enough to confront the difficulties of marriage and fatherhood. I had lost the innocence that life in a small town was supposed to preserve.

Yet I had rebounded from the depths of spring. I was beginning to form a plan. I told no friends about my situation but I confided in the teachers who had most changed my life: Mr. Ross, Mrs. Wilson, and Professor Taylor. I could still scout with my former coach, he said. Mrs. Wilson claimed that I was the best student she had ever taught. I should continue to study and become a teacher. "Lizzie, you would be a natural in the classroom." Professor Taylor said, "You have an aptitude for philosophy. Someday you will have the ability to do graduate work." The obstacles I would face could be surmounted. My teachers were there to help me in any way they could. Shortly after arriving in Oklahoma City I received the first of many letters from each teacher, correspondence that would encourage and sustain me for the difficult years ahead.

The fields were post-harvest brown and flat when we left Conway. We headed for a place where the landscape was green and the hills began to roll as we neared the City. I was unsure what life had in store for me. My 1936 Martin D-18 was in the backseat.

EPILOGUE

I named him Chance: Chance Tucker, no middle name. Until I legally changed his name to Chance Ware. At some point there was no longer any Tucker interest in the life and destiny of my son – no absent father or concerned grandmother to keep a family spark alive. There was just Chance and Lizzie Ware – the other name was no longer significant.

I decided not to give up my baby for adoption. It was irresponsible to let others do what I ought to do. And the biological bonds between mother and son, as he was developing inside of me, became profoundly powerful. The grandparents agreed to help support a single mother and their grandchild: $100 a month from each family, not much, but we didn't need much. Aunt Joan and Uncle Virgil were wonderful to me: kind, sensitive, loving. My garage apartment provided some privacy and time to read – at least until November 15, 1968, when Chance arrived. My mother came for a week to help and to instruct. Pastor Fred was much too busy to make the trip to see my little *bastard.* That unfortunate "slip of his tongue" was made before I left Conway; merely the Preacher's reference to illegitimacy, not an act of cussing.

Jake came for two awkward days at Thanksgiving -- the beginning of the end. He talked and talked about OSU and the baseball team and his classes. He had very little to do with

Chance. A dirty diaper was beyond his capabilities. We slept in separate bedrooms; our kisses and embraces were more like the behavior of close friends than lovers. We tried again at Christmas vacation but the atmosphere was even more strained. His final exams were in the first week of the new year. He had to rush back to Conway to study: calculus, chemistry, and something else. Great to see you, he said. I may be back for spring break. It depends on whether I make the travel squad. We play in Arizona in March. Not a word about a possible future together. I wondered whether OSU coeds were pleasant distractions.

The news from Stillwater next spring was not encouraging for Jake's baseball career. He didn't make the travel team. He suited up for home games, along with the other scrubs, but scarcely played. His Division I career ended with two innings played in the field, one at bat, and one pinch running appearance. Vera thought he was being treated unfairly by the head coach because he came from a small school.

I saw him briefly in the beginning of June. He played on a summer team of college players in Wichita and commuted to the farm for harvest and to work the fields. He was too involved to see me or his son. The letter in August, before the start of the fall term, was unsurprising. He had talked to the baseball coach at Great Plains State College. He would play baseball and major in Mathematics Education. He would be a teacher, coach, and farmer, just as we had talked about when we were pondering our futures together. *And, oh by the way Lizzie, I don't think I love you anymore. I'm not ready to be a father and I met this other girl....I talked to my mom,* he wrote. *She will keep sending you a check until you get on your feet. Good luck. Have a good life.*

The big news in the spring was that Pastor Fred had requested and accepted another church assignment back in Missouri, home for my father and mother. In Conway I was an embarrassment who caused him shame. In small town Missouri I was simply a daughter who lived in Oklahoma City with Uncle Virgil and Aunt Joan. No need to mention a child born out of wedlock. If I had wanted to visit Conway there was no place to stay. My life had a feeling of uncanniness. I was no longer at home because I no longer had a home: the pink parsonage, a room of my own, the streets of Conway, the fields I worked, the pastures I tromped with Jake, the country roads I walked.

When I left Conway Josh's baseball future was uncertain. John told the Yankees' scout he would seriously consider their offer but it took only a day for a decision to be made. Jesus Christ defeated the New York Yankees. They came back the following spring, after Josh had turned eighteen years old, with a higher offer: a $15,000 bonus to sign. As an adult he could have defied his father's wishes and insisted that throwing a baseball with the intention of helping his team defeat an opponent would not undermine his Christian character. But he couldn't do it. In the fall after graduation he had been hired by the fire department in Alma. The irony wasn't lost on me. He chose to be a fireman in real life, never to be a fireman on the baseball field, putting out rallies and saving his fellow teammates in a world of competitive play. He married, had a family, and moved from Alma to take a promotion in another fire department, in a town near Tulsa where Ruth lived. He left the Christian Scientist Church but he remained an unchurched Christian, a fine man and athlete, until cancer felled him. Josh was gifted, but religion robbed him of his gift.

Jake's second year in college took an unlucky turn on December 1, 1969, the year of the United States Selective Service draft lottery, the first Vietnam draft lottery. He was in the fifth most unlucky group of young men that night. He didn't have to wait long for his birth date to be called: October 18, draft slot 005. Another chance had entered his life and this time it was lethal randomness. Gamblers' wisdom at the time claimed that luck would be distributed in thirds: the first basket of birthdates would be drafted; the second third of young men were in moderate danger; the last third would be safe. The first 195 birthdates were later drafted, in the order they were drawn.

Jake finished his year at GPSC. In the spring he shared second base with an older player. He became what he was projected to be: a solid small college baseball player who might become an all-conference performer as an upperclassman – but not a pro prospect. He could have retained his student deferment until he graduated, but there were credible rumors that deferments would be changed. Students would be able to postpone the inevitable only until finishing the term in which they were enrolled. This happened in 1971.

Perhaps Jake's patriotism got the better of him. Anti-war rallies hadn't reached the campus of Great Plains State College. He could serve, then finish his degree (and play baseball) after the completion of his two-year obligation. He joined the Army after harvest, his fitness made him an excellent recruit for the infantry, and he shipped out to Vietnam in late fall. On the first day of spring in 1971, on a lovely baseball day in Oklahoma, he was killed in action. Vera was devastated. Soon the checks stopped, with no explanation, and she slowly drank herself to death.

I re-read my favorite passages from *My Antonia* on the first day of each new spring. They are passages about the plains landscape, the passing seasons, and the "precious, the incommunicable past." For me Cather is not writing about her fictional Black Hawk nor about the real Red Cloud, Nebraska. She is writing about Conway. I superimpose my memories onto her descriptions. In my mind I replace her red prairie grass with the sea of brilliant wheat that undulates just before harvest. Her skies and seasons are like mine and I let her speak for me about our relationship to the past.

I regret so many things about Jake's early death. I think he may have grown into being a father even if his relationship to his son would have been a long-distance job. Jake would have traveled to some of Chance's baseball games and gleamed like Vera at the prospects of his son's developing talents. The father would have been so proud when Chance signed his first professional contract, and he would have been pleased when the son became a high school mathematics teacher and baseball coach after his minor league playing career. I regret the absence of Conway in my son's life. I imagine Chance visiting the farm, riding on the combine with his father, tasting the dust as he circled the fields on a tractor, bucking alfalfa bales in a barn loft, and watching a massive thunderstorm approach from the west in the big sky. And I regret not being able to share with Jake the incommunicable past that we possessed together.

Most of the important people from my Conway years are now dead. Some I loved, others I respected and admired. Pastor Fred and I never reconciled. I was a willing daughter but the relationship was frigid. He never visited and he didn't ask about my plans. My mother was pleased when I began to take classes at an Oklahoma City junior college, but she was perplexed when I transferred to the University of Oklahoma to major in Letters, following the path of Professor Enos Taylor.

Chance and I visited small town Missouri for holidays. My father and I had icy conversations about the Cardinals, but I was sure Pastor Fred was relieved when we left and he could get back to saving other, more winnable, souls. He no longer asked whether I prayed or about the inner workings of my relationship with Jesus Christ, my personal savior. Had he given up on my soul?

After I left Conway, Coach Ross insisted that I call him "Bill," which didn't seem right to me, so we compromised. He became "Coach Bill." For a few years I remained a bird-dog for a bird-dog, looking for a boy in the bushes, another Josh or maybe even a Mickey. I took Chance to games where we sat with Coach Bill and scouted together, comparing stopwatch times. An attempted steal and the catcher pegs to second. Coach Bill looks at his stopwatch as I look at mine. I ask, "What did you get?"

"2.1. Not bad, but he's no Johnny Bench."

When Chance was older, I bought a stopwatch for him so we could scout together. After retirement Coach Bill returned to northeast Oklahoma, to the Cherokee Nation, and scouted until he died.

My Norman years were full and intense, like Jim Burden's time at a northern Great Plains university, before he went east to study law. My inheritance from Harry helped to pay for tuition, daycare, and a modest rent for a slum near the campus. I worked part-time and was constantly sleep-deprived, but I had the sense that Chance and I were surviving and on the way. I saw Marcia a few times but she was involved with sorority things and uninterested in classes required for my major: literature, philosophy, history. For her, Chance was a novelty.

Professor Taylor was right. I had an aptitude for philosophy – as well as languages. I excelled in Classical Greek. And Norman provided cultural life. One memorable evening I took Chance to a nearby campus bar, jazz on Wednesday nights instead of rock and roll. There was Al Little, playing Bill Evans.

My correspondence with Mrs. Wilson and Professor Taylor during those years was regular and important. Mrs. Wilson, now teaching at Great Plains State College, was excited when I began graduate work in philosophy, although she had hoped I would study literature. To celebrate admission to the graduate program and my assistantship award, Professor Taylor sent me signed copies of four books by Gustav Mueller: *Discourses on Religion* (1951), *Plato, The Founder of Philosophy as Dialectic* (1965); *Hegel, The Man, His Vision and His Work* (1970); and *Instead of a Biography* (1970). The last title contained a charming account of Professor Mueller's experiences in the Philosophy Department at OU and life in Norman from 1930 until he left in 1968. He lived in a large pink house called "Big Pink" on Jenkins Street, near the football stadium -- his own pink parsonage.

In graduate school I came under the influence of two people: an older male scholar of ancient philosophy, and a young, recently hired specialist on Wittgenstein. She was the first full-time tenure track female in the department, and she encouraged me to continue studying philosophy. As a graduate assistant I was assigned to grade for her introductory courses and teach Friday recitation sections. She said I was a natural in the classroom. Mrs. Wilson had been prescient.

I finished an M.A. in philosophy in three years. We headed east, like Jim Burden, for a Ph.D program in a big city, where I specialized in ancient philosophy and coaching Chance in Baseball 101.

I'm nearing retirement and nearer to death. I gave up the chance to play for The Flying Queens and to make a life on the Great Plains, but our life has gone well. After finishing the Ph.D and writing a dissertation on ancient stoicism I was hired at a state university in the west, in an intelligent college town with a good youth baseball program, tucked into the foothills of the Rocky Mountains – the first female tenure track faculty member in the philosophy department, a specialist in Ancient Philosophy and Ethics. I have done what academic philosophers do: teach courses, write books and articles few read, and become involved in academic politics, in which the disputes are bitter because the stakes are so low. I have dazzled colleagues and friends with my athletic talents outside the classroom, on intramural basketball courts and recreational softball fields. I have thrown more batting practice to a son than any mother in the history of baseball – and I have been a good mother.

There were two ruling passions in Pastor Fred's life: Jesus Christ and the St. Louis Cardinals. The former caused the unraveling of our relationship. He was ashamed and embarrassed by the existence of my son. He was horrified that I no longer accepted Jesus Christ as my personal savior. He was ignorant about and uninterested in my study of philosophy. He was distraught that I didn't seek the answers to my questions in the Bible. And there were other aspects of my life that left him disgusted. Overall, he thought my life was a failure and my eternal destiny dismal. But I still love the Cardinals.

I seldom returned to Conway, yet I have returned often in my mind, when I play my 1936 Martin D-18, or listen to Bill Evans, or attempt to write a poem in the style of Walt Whitman, when the images and impressions of northwest Oklahoma in the 1960s pursue me, against my will, become alive, and crowd out the present. I think about the mysteries of late life and the magic of Josh's gift – his fastball's late life – and Jake's early death, and what might have been.

ACKNOWLEDGEMENTS

I would like to thank Mallory Young for pointing me in the direction of Fine Dog Press. As usual, her instincts and good judgment were important for helping me to make the connection that ultimately led to this book being published.

I had the good fortune to have two fine editors work with me, one literally in-house, the other at Fine Dog Press. Of course, my in-house editor, Barb, my wife for over fifty years, was more than an editor. There are parts of this book that could not have been written without her contributions. She provided gallons of encouragement, wise suggestions at crucial points, and insights whose genesis came more from her experiences than mine. The book is hers, also.

I have thoroughly enjoyed my collaboration with Roxie Faulkner Kirk at Fine Dog Press. There is no doubt that the book is better because of her thoughtful comments, criticisms, and suggestions. She had a keen knack for seeing weaknesses and forcing me to dig deeper in depicting scenes and relationships. Only an accomplished writer in her own right could have done what she did for this book. Thanks, Roxie.

Randolph Feezell grew up on a small wheat farm in northwest Oklahoma, graduated from a tiny country high school, played baseball at the University of Oklahoma, and became a college teacher, academic philosopher, and baseball coach. He holds a Ph.D in philosophy from State University of New York at Buffalo. He is the author of several books, including Beyond the Fields: A Cherokee Strip Farm, a Baseball Life, and the Love of Wisdom (a memoir); The ABCs of Trump: Asshole, Bullshitter, Chauvinist, Essays on Life in Trumpworld; and four philosophical books about sport. He lives in the West with his wife, Barb, and still owns 160 acres of red dirt in Woods County, Oklahoma. This is his first novel.